Alexander Ikonnikov was born in 1974 in the Russian town of Urshum near Kirov on Lake Viatka. Having finished his German studies, Ikonnikow was due to do military service. This had little appeal for him – this was during the war in Afghanistan – so he chose the civilian option. He became an English teacher without knowing a word of English in Bystritza, and after a two-year stint he escaped to Kirov. There he worked as a journalist, a job he gave up to devote himself to writing fulltime. *Lizka and Her Men* is the first of Ikonnikov's works to be translated into English.

LIZKA AND HER MEN

Alexander Ikonnikov

Translated by Andrew Bromfield

A complete catalogue record for this book can be
obtained from the British Library on request

Originally published under the title *Liska Und Ihre Männer*
Copyright ©2003 by Rowohlt Verlag, Reinbek bei Hamburg

Translation copyright ©2007 Andrew Bromfield

First published in 2007 by Serpent's Tail,
an imprint of Profile Books Ltd
3A Exmouth House
Pine Street
London EC1R OJH
website: www.serpentstail.com

Designed and typeset at Neuadd Bwll, Llanwrtyd Wells

Printed in the UK by CPI Bookmarque, Croydon, CR0 4TD

10   9   8   7   6   5   4   3   2   1

ȢNE

THE SMALL TOWN of Lopukhov, located amid the picturesque landscapes of the central region of Russia, was little different from thousands of other such provincial towns in the pre-war period. Narrow, dusty little streets with countless packs of stray dogs, squalid little houses with tumbledown fences, chickens and geese strolling calmly around the main square and a church without a cross on its dome, converted with careless haste into a granary. Since olden times Lopukhov had been inhabited by Listievs, Kapustins, Travkins and, of course, Lopukhovs. There were also Ivanovs, Petrovs and Sidorovs living here, as well as families with a couple of hundred other Russian surnames, but there weren't any Ogurtsovs: the first bearer of that name appeared in a most unusual manner.

On the 1st of October 1939 the ears of the local inhabitants were assaulted by an incredible roaring sound coming from old Semyonovskaya Street, the town's only paved thoroughfare, mingled with the shouts of children and the shrilling of a militiaman's whistle. The curious citizens – including the young seamstress Sveta – hurried to the source of the noise and there, for the first time in their lives, they saw an automobile. Belching out clouds of smoke, the light truck was bounding furiously from one end of the street to the other and back, pursued by an excited gang of young boys. There was a red-faced, sweaty militiaman running in front of it, blowing feverishly on his whistle, waving his arms about to disperse the people walking in the street and shouting: "Make way! Make way!"

The truck was driven by a handsome young man with dark hair, a moustache and a haughty air. He was completely drunk. His flying goggles and leather helmet and the smell of petrol made such a great impression on Sveta that she pushed her way through the crowd and darted out into the road, almost ending up under the truck. The driver braked sharply and their eyes met, but he didn't swear, he simply held his hand out to Sveta and invited her to get into the cab.

All day long they drove round the town, gaped at by envious idlers, and in the evening they strolled along the dark lanes of the town's park, where he told her about pistons and cylinders, and she sighed languorously, until eventually she invited him to stay the night with her.

Driver Ogurtsov may have been a soldier, but he was also a man of honour. The following morning he and Sveta went to the registry office, and in the evening of the same day he left for the Finnish border and never came back again.

Nine months later Vladimir Ogurtsov made his appearance. He grew up a sickly boy, and the hungry war years undermined his health still further. In addition to sewing soldiers' greatcoats and caring for the wounded, Sveta also had to work in the forestry, felling timber, in order somehow to increase the amount of their rations. In the winter of 1944 she died following a serious illness and the boy was taken into state care, in an already overcrowded orphanage. Bread made from rotten potatoes and soup made from goosefoot leaves, relentless studying and exhausting labour, side-by-side with the women and the German prisoners, to rebuild the life that had been destroyed by the war, tempered his character and developed his fighting spirit. The height of Vladimir's childhood dreams, and the dreams of all his barefoot peers, was a pair of box calf boots. His dream came true: he became an army officer and after that he never took them off again.

After graduating from a military college in one of the USSR's secret cities, Vladimir was given ninety days' leave and he came to Lopukhov. After visiting his old haunts and his mother's grave, he made his way to the dance in the town park, where he was unable to resist the blazing eyes of Elena Georgievna, a young girl from a nearby village. After those first three months of tenderness and passion, the modest and pretty Elena Georgievna saw her husband only three more times in her life. The first time he came in 1968 to allow the bullet wound in his leg to heal, and left after six months for one of the USSR's secret wars. The second time he came back was in 1970, and they had a daughter, Liza. The third time was in 1972, when he came to recover from concussion and to help his wife around the house and the vegetable garden. After that Vladimir Ogurtsov disappeared. Elena Georgievna cried for a long time and even wrote several letters to the Minister of Defence, but none of them were answered.

"Where's our daddy?" three-year-old Lizka used to ask.

"At the war, my little daughter."

"But we're not at war with anyone!" five-year-old Lizka used to exclaim.

"But our country has a lot of friends and we have to help them."

"And why haven't I ever seen these friends?" the seven-year-old girl used to ask.

But Elena Georgievna didn't answer, she just went away into their room and cried quietly, pretending to be reading a book.

Every month she went to the Lopukhov military registration and records office, hoping that they would tell her something about her husband, and if he'd been dead she could have counted on receiving his pension and a comfortable apartment. But they didn't know anything, and Elena Georgievna and her little daughter had to carry on huddling together in one room of a communal apartment in a half-rotten barracks building. Since she had no education, she tried working as a night-nurse in the local hospital, until she realised she couldn't raise Lizka on that kind of meagre income.

But she was still young and beautiful, and men began to appear in her life. The first was the director of the vegetable depot, and so Elena Georgievna didn't have to bother herself with keeping an allotment like all the other Soviet citizens in Lopukhov. On Tuesdays and Fridays the deputy director of the meat combine came to visit, always leaving the refrigerator full of ham and choice sorts of sausage when he left. But the one little Lizka liked most of all was the director of the local market, who always brought a green watermelon or yellow melon with him, and sometimes even peaches and the one item that was in the shortest supply of all in the Soviet Union – bananas.

The local kids on the block, who used to tease Lizka for having no father, were instantly silenced, because now when they asked her where her dad was, she replied proudly that she had several dads. Out in the yard and at kindergarten Lizka avoided the other girls, because she thought they were sissies. She despised their games and preferred kicking a ball around with the boys. Thanks to her hot temper and independent character, she never had any problems standing up for herself and she cheerfully joined in all the children's fights. Nobody ever called her Liza, let alone Elizaveta, the name that was on her birth certificate. Even her teachers, weary of battling against her stubborn resistance, got used to the humble form of "Lizka".

The number of Elena Georgievna's visitors constantly increased, and Lizka was left to her own devices the whole day long. Every summer she was given a new bicycle and every winter new skis. Her mother made every possible effort to conceal her trade from her daughter, which meant she did everything she could to ensure that her daughter spent as much time as possible outside. Lizka's favourite haunt was in the fruit orchards: blossoming and fragrant in spring, covered with a soft carpet of bright-coloured leaves in the autumn and dressed in whimsical snowy caps in the winter – she could complain to them about a harsh word from her mother, share her loneliness with them or simply dream.

And then the time came to go to school and, like all other Soviet children, Lizka woke to the strains of the state hymn on the radio, put on her red young pioneer's tie and went to the Lopukhov school where, in addition to reading, writing and maths, she was taught how to take a Kalashnikov automatic rifle to pieces, use a gas mask and hide from American bombs in the basement. Lizka did not demonstrate any particular aptitudes in her studies and, regardless of whether she made an effort or not, most of her marks were average. The only subject in which she got "good" and "excellent" was physics. That was because Lizka fell in love with the physics teacher – an intelligent and independent woman who always smelled of tobacco – and tried to imitate everything about her. Elena Georgievna had even begun to hope that her daughter was not so devoid of talent after all, but the physics teacher soon left and Lizka's interest in science faded away, leaving her with nothing but a smoking habit.

Lizka eventually began to feel that she was going through certain changes. Suddenly for no reason her body would start to ache sweetly, and sometimes a light tremor would run through it if one of her classmates accidentally touched her during the break or in the P.E. class. Several times she found herself frankly staring wide-eyed at the figures of her female classmates in the changing-room and the gym. Her cheeks blazed bright red, and she got a heavy feeling in her breasts, but she couldn't stop herself looking at them like that.

When her mother wasn't at home, Lizka would take her clothes off and look at herself in the mirror. She was trying to decide if she was beautiful or not, but she couldn't give a definite answer to her own question. She studied her face, putting her hand over her forehead or nose or chin by turns. Taken separately, they looked beautiful to her, but in combination they somehow seemed very ugly and they didn't suit her brown eyes and chestnut hair at all. The main cause of her dissatisfaction was her breasts, which were so small that Lizka resorted to cunning: she sewed some shoulder pads she had torn out of her mother's old jackets into her bra. The only thing she felt proud of was her legs, and she took pleasure in demonstrating how slim and elegant they were to the people around her by shortening her already high dresses and skirts even further.

Legs like these could not possibly fail to be noticed by the boys from the senior classes. They hooted and whistled after her and made dirty wisecracks, but she never reacted to them and just strode on proudly with her head held high. Lizka kept herself apart from the others; she didn't make any close friends among the boys or the girls, and if you didn't count the stoker Pasha, she was almost a complete solitary.

The boiler room where this retiring, taciturn young man of twenty-five worked happened to lie on Lizka's way from home to school, and she called in there almost every day to have a secret smoke and watch Pasha flinging the coal into the immense furnaces with his big shovel. Pasha's bare torso, the flames and the steam boilers aroused in her a mysterious longing for that thing that the other girls whispered about most of the time during the breaks; some of them even confessed that they'd already tried it and described it in great detail. And when this mysterious, unfamiliar, frightening but alluring feeling turned into desire and became unbearable, he was the one she chose as the most appropriate man.

That evening she told her mother she was going to a girlfriend's birthday party, bought a bottle of fortified port with money she'd saved from her school dinners and went to see Pasha. The young stoker was embarrassed at first, but then he invited Lizka into his small box-room, where there was a narrow bed and a little table covered with coal dust.

Pasha gulped his wine down fast, following it with pieces of salami, and he got drunk very quickly. After half a bottle his shifty eyes began to glitter in his dirty face and he even tried to tell her something funny. But Lizka wasn't listening to him, she just smoked without saying anything and thought about how it would feel when those sooty hands touched her white body. And then she got undressed, dived under the blanket and began watching to see what Pasha would do.

He put down his piece of sausage, wiped his hands on the curtain and began getting undressed too. The zip on one of his boots stuck and he couldn't get it open, so he fell on Lizka with it still on and his trousers down round one ankle.

It all happened so fast that she didn't feel a thing apart from the pain and a sensation of something dirty inside her.

"And that's what people shoot themselves in the head for, and slash their veins, and write poems and don't sleep at night?" she thought on her way home. "Oh no. I'm never going to love anyone."

She looked at her mother, who had had so many men in her life, with completely different eyes now. She couldn't understand her behaving like that, it seemed absolutely incredible.

But although Lizka found the idea of being in bed with a man repulsive and frightening, she liked the feeling that she was a woman now. She allowed Yurka from the tenth class to take her to the cinema twice, and once she made such provocative eyes at the P.E. teacher that he blushed and hastily turned away. Young men instantly began to feel attracted, sensing the startling change in her and she enjoyed toying with them and being the focus of general attention. In her mind Lizka divided them into two categories: primitive spotty juveniles who were only good for flirting with, and the more grown-up and dignified ones, who smelled of eau-de-cologne and tobacco, with whom she could stroll arm-in-arm without feeling ashamed and make her girlfriends jealous.

But what delighted Lizka most of all was that Alexei, the most noteworthy and most handsome boy in the school, began taking an admiring interest in her. He was a star pupil, a sportsman and secretary of the school's branch of the Communist Youth League. How insanely happy she was when he invited her to parties at his place, wrote her little love letters in class and saw her home in the evening after school. Even the teachers who complained to Elena Georgievna that her daughter didn't wear the compulsory school uniform, used make-up and made no effort to become an active member of communist society, approved of this alliance. And perhaps everything would have been all right, if only one week before the final exams Pasha had not decided to boast to all his friends that he had taken Lizka's virginity.

Lizka had quite simply never expected that this quiet, retiring stoker could do such a thing. The entire rumour-hungry little town exploded in a mad fit of vilification. Heads in Lopukhov began shaking reproachfully, eyes began looking askance, her admirers turned their backs on her, and their words echoed round and round in Lizka's brain: "The whore! Following in her mother's footsteps. She's the same kind of whore as her mother."

Lizka would run to the fruit orchards and take deep breaths of the warm spring air so that she wouldn't burst into tears, and lie there for a long time, devastated and absolutely still, on the fresh grass. For the first time she told her mother about her grief, and for a while she even felt there was no more distance between them, but she was wrong. Elena Georgievna looked at her with kind, loving eyes that didn't understand a thing. But Lizka could read that word "whore" in the faces of her classmates, who whispered behind her back, and on the faces of her teachers, who pretended that they were unbiased and nothing had happened, and on the faces of the old female pensioners, who had grown into the bench in the yard, and on the faces of everyone she knew or didn't know who passed her in the street. Wretched, provincial Lopukhov was slowly devouring her.

Lizka hadn't given any thought to her future profession as yet, but luckily for her just at this time the medical college in the city of G. announced that it would accept the school graduation exams as equivalent to its entrance exams and she immediately grabbed at this opportunity, deciding that even being a nurse was better than staying here for one more day. And while her class was having fun at the graduation ball, Lizka took the two heavy suitcases she had packed and a letter for her aunt, whom she had never seen, and set out for G.

"Goodbye, Mum! Goodbye, home town! Goodbye, loathsome, pitiful Lopukhov!"

TWO

LIZKA SPENT ALL the way from the station to her aunt's house with her face glued to the window of the tram, curiously watching the people bustling about. Following some inexplicable logic, they went dashing along past the standard boxes of the buildings, ran across the streets in large crowds, rushed into places and rushed back out again. The four-lane streets were packed solid with cars and buses constantly honking their horns and piling up into traffic jams. And when the tram drove up on to the bridge, the entire city of G. was laid out before Lizka's eyes in all its glory. Extending along both sides of the river, its developments reached almost to the very horizon, where dozens, maybe even hundreds, of factory chimneys belched smoke into the sky.

Lizka had to walk quite a distance from the tram stop and she made frequent halts to rest her arms from the weight of the suitcases. She involuntarily compared herself with the city people, astounded that they could move about so lightly and independently, that no one said hello to anyone else, that they were dressed so elegantly. Although Lizka was dressed in the best that she had, she was ashamed to look so provincial. She gazed into the faces of passers-by, as if she were trying to see what they thought of her – were they approving or critical? – but they were all hurrying about their own business and not paying any attention at all to her.

Her aunt, an elderly woman with ginger hair, wearing a kimono, greeted her niece rather coolly. After inviting Lizka inside, she began reading Elena Georgievna's letter and her expression became more and more hostile.

"A strange woman," Lizka thought, glancing round the apartment. There were basins full of water standing on the floor, the parquet flooring was covered with scrapes from furniture being moved about and there were bells, large and small, hanging everywhere.

"You know, you can't live with us," the aunt said eventually, and she made a circle round Lizka's head as she continued. "You radiate negative energy. That could damage the aura of our dwelling."

"I beg your pardon?" Lizka asked, puzzled.

"My husband and I hold an esoteric view of the world. We have spent so long seeking unity with the spirit that we are afraid of any kind of external interference. But don't you worry, we'll find you a place to live. My husband knows the supervisor of one of the student hostels in the workers' quarter, and that's not far from your medical college." Her aunt waved her hand through the air again. "Anyway, you can stay here tonight. But go and take a walk now, I have to do my breathing exercises."

As she wandered aimlessly around the unfamiliar city, examining the shop windows and spending her mother's meagre savings on cakes in almost every delicatessen, Lizka pondered her present situation. Although the reception from her only relative made her feel offended and rather sorry for herself, in her heart she rejoiced at her total freedom. Nobody in this city knew her or her mother, and now she had a chance to start a new, completely different life of her own.

The student hostel that was going to be Lizka's home was an old four-storey prefabricated building from Khrushchev's days with the plaster falling off its walls. As she walked inside, Lizka caught a sharp smell of urine and fried onions. There were somebody's children running around in the semi-darkness of the corridor, two women with saucepans in their hands were quarrelling loudly, and the open windows were filled with drying laundry, so that hardly any sunlight or fresh air could percolate through it.

When Lizka found her room, she was surprised to find that three other girls were already living in it.

"Hello," she said from the doorway and showed them her warrant. "They've put me in with you."

"Oh, that's going too far!" one of the girls said indignantly, tossing aside the book she had just been reading.

"And where do you think we're supposed to put the bed?" another girl enquired in outrage.

"That's enough of that!" said the oldest girl, getting up to meet Lizka and holding out her hand. "My name's Nina, this is Vika and this is Olga. Come in, we'll think of some way to manage the bed."

The room really was too small for four people. There were three beds set along the walls, with a large wardrobe separating them from a table that evidently served for preparing food and carrying out study assignments at the same time. From the books standing on the shelves and the windowsill, Lizka immediately realised that the girls were also studying in the medical college. The bedside locker that she was given was missing a leg, and its place had been taken by textbooks on Latin and the immobilisation of road transport. While Vika and Olga were clearing a space in the cupboard with a disgruntled air and Lizka was laying out her things there, Nina solved the problem of where to put another bed. The girls hammered nails through the plastic feet on the legs of one bed, stood it on top of another and hammered the nails into the wooden headboards of the lower bed. This two-storey structure turned out to be rather sturdy, but even so Lizka, as the youngest, found herself sleeping on top.

"All right then, the more the merrier," Nina said, when the installation of the newcomer had been completed. "Now it's time for the housewarming." She took a bottle of medical spirit out from under her bed and mixed it with diluted raspberry juice. After all the girls had taken a swallow from the large aluminium mug, they burst into laughter, and the final trace left of Lizka's original chilly reception was dispelled.

During the conversations that followed, Lizka realised that Nina was the leader in this room. She had graduated from the college two years earlier and now she worked in a dermato-venerological clinic. In her search for living space and a husband she was wavering between two admirers. One was an engineer with a car, but with no living space of his own, the other was an architect with no car but with an old grandmother who had left him her apartment in her will. Unable to decide which of them to choose, Nina was dating both of them, and sometimes she dated the plumber Tolya from the next room as well. Vika and Olga were not much older than Lizka and they were in the second year at the college. They assured her that studying at the medical college wasn't hard at all; the main thing was to survive the first year, and they would find her a suitable boyfriend.

The housewarming party had to be broken off suddenly to deal with an unforeseen emergency. For some unknown reason the upper floors had decided to organise a general cockroach hunt. The panic-stricken insects were escaping by running along the central heating pipes and through the ventilation and electric wiring ducts. They came creeping out of every possible crack and cranny, and entire colonies of them swarmed along the corridor, hiding in the cupboards and refrigerators and dropping off the ceiling right on to people's heads. In order to keep these repulsive creatures out of their room, the girls were also obliged to resort to poisonous insecticide and chemical chalk. It became quite impossible to breathe in the hostel and so the girls hurried outside.

As well as their little group, there were a lot of other people out there. The tipsy young workers and students strolled about in vests and tracksuit trousers with baggy knees, bawling out songs to the strumming of guitars and swearing obscenely. Since, as a rule, everyone ran out of rationing coupons for hard liquor by the middle of the month, they were making do with moonshine and home brew. Lizka wasn't used to strong drinks and she wanted to refuse, but she was afraid of seeming different from all the others. After her first mouthful of some sickly sweet liquid, she felt she was going to puke immediately and made a dash for the bushes. Nina came across her. "Would you like some advice?"

"What?" Lizka stuck two fingers down her throat and puked.

"Get out of this lousy dump before it's too late. Otherwise you'll end up stuck here like a total idiot and wind up marrying some absolute jerk. You can't imagine how furious I get at living in all this filth and having to queue for the shower. In winter, when the toilet breaks down, everybody goes in the back yard, wherever they like. You can't see the shit now, because when the snow melts we all put in a day's work to clear it. It's impossible to live here. It's up to you, but I beg you, get out of here quick!"

Lizka was so dumbfounded that she immediately stopped being sick. She'd thought her new roommates were perfectly happy to be all together in such a cheerful group. She gaped at Nina in amazement.

"Then why do you live here?"

"Because I used to be just the same kind of fool as you are. And also because I'll be getting married soon and I'll leave this slum for ever. I'm tired of asking the girls to hang about in the corridor for half an hour if I have a boyfriend over. And the way the bed creaks and everyone in the next room howls with laughter! My God, if only I could be seventeen again. Get out before it's too late."

"But I need time," Lizka objected. "I want to take a look around and see what's what."

"Rubbish! You don't need any time. Believe me, you'll sink up to your throat in this quagmire, and when you try to pull yourself out it will already be pouring into your mouth. Look for a job and a room. I don't want you to suffer like the rest of us do here. And meanwhile you can wear my old shoes. Yours are absolutely no good for anything," said Nina and kissed her on the cheek with a smile.

That evening the girls arranged a little excursion for Lizka, in the course of which she learned at what time and on which days she could use the shower and the electrical cooker in the communal kitchen. She was also introduced to some of their neighbours from the other rooms. There were students and workers, married couples and bachelors, and there were so many of them that she couldn't remember all their names. That night, with her head full of new impressions, feeling as if she had known all these people for a long time, she fell into a calm and happy sleep.

The next day the girls selflessly devoted themselves to Lizka's appearance, since tomorrow would be her first day in college. While Vika gave her a short haircut in the latest fashion from the magazine *Working Woman*, Nina and Olga rummaged through both her suitcases until they came to the conclusion that they ought to have been much lighter. The underwear from Lopukhov provoked such hearty laughter that Lizka blushed in embarrassment. But in the girls' opinion, something could still be done with the other things. They themselves also bought their clothes in Soviet shops, but they reworked almost all their dresses, skirts and blouses themselves, because the sewing workshop was beyond their means.

On the one hand, they wanted Lizka to look her absolute best and appear before her future fellow-students in all her splendour, but on the other hand, there was a certain danger of incurring the displeasure of Hobgoblin, the head of the medical faculty. As an old maid with puritanical views and Stalinist training, she absolutely hated female students who radiated youth and beauty. The girls lent Lizka a few of their own things and dressed her up so that she could hardly recognise herself in the mirror, and the next day she walked proudly and confidently along the corridors of her new place of study, freed from her provincial inferiority complex. However, that did not save her from a clash with Hobgoblin.

"Well then, you idle blockheads, you've been lucky. You are part of our new experimental programme, which will require determined application on your part. During the summer you will do an accelerated course, in August you will have a break for holidays and in September the usual academic year will begin." The head of faculty cast a chilly glance at her audience and smiled in an odd, metallic kind of way. "And remember, you crowd of loafers, this is not school, where they used to coddle you like little children."

A buzz of resentment ran round the hall. Offended by such a hostile attitude, the students were sharing their first impressions of Hobgoblin.

"Silence!" she exclaimed in a shrill voice and struck her pointer hard against her chair. "I would like to remind you that the rules of discipline remain in force. I shall have something special to say to those who skip classes and are fond of make-up, short skirts and cigarettes. And now, my little sluts, open your exercise books and write down the weekly timetable."

"No one gave you any right to insult us." Lizka's voice sounded uncertain, but it was loud. She surprised even herself by getting up and saying those words.

"Your surname, my dear?" Hobgoblin asked almost affectionately.

"Ogurtsova."

"I shall be paying very close attention to your progress, comrade Ogurtsova. *Unum castigabis – centum ementabis*."

When Lizka's roommates heard about what had happened they warned her that next time a similar situation came up it would be better to keep quiet. They cited several examples of how Hobgoblin had dealt with those she had taken a dislike to. The head of faculty had excluded one student, who had fallen in love with her *Docent*, simply for wearing lipstick and mascara, even though she got top grades in everything. And she had refused to allow another student to sit an exam because her absence from two lectures had not been justified by a doctor's certificate. Even the lecturers who knew Hobgoblin well had been afraid to intervene for the poor girl.

A week later, Lizka already knew what it felt like to be in disgrace. Hobgoblin refused to say hello to her, checked her answers to the numerous tests more closely than the other girls', and every time Lizka wanted to go outside for a smoke, she followed her out on to the porch, so that Lizka had to pretend she was taking a breath of fresh air.

The terrible living conditions, the constant drinking binges in the hostel, which prevented Lizka from concentrating on her studies, and the head of faculty's special attention soon set her thinking about what Nina had said. And although most places only hired students with great reluctance, Lizka was lucky.

The head of the housing department read Lizka's application, studied her passport closely and nodded. "Well, we need yard-keepers. There's plenty of work to do. Your pay's not very high, of course, but you can count on ninety roubles. Off you go to the house manager, he'll give you the brushes and spade and all the rest. Here's the address."

The object of Lizka's future efforts, house number 18 on the Street of the Athletes, was an ordinary panel-built nine-storey apartment block, standing alone in the middle of an empty lot overgrown with tall weeds. In front of the house there was a children's playground, tightly surrounded by a ring of maple trees, and a large parking lot, with an old Pobeda standing in the corner on four props instead of wheels.

After receiving her equipment and the keys to the closet from the house manager, Lizka sat on one of the children's swings in the yard and looked around. Some noisy kids were kicking a ball around between two goals improvised out of bricks, the old women on the benches by the entrances were mulling over their interminable gossip and several men had settled comfortably in the shade of the trees with their cards and beer. Lizka imagined how all these people would stare at her if she started swinging her broom right there and then. And although her mother had often told her that whatever kind of work anyone did, there was nothing shameful about it, Lizka felt uneasy somehow. What would they think about her when they saw her in the ugly yard-keeper's coat with a scraper in her hands?

Her thoughts were interrupted by the appearance of a truck from the direction of the empty lot. Huge lumps of mud fell off its wheels on to the asphalt of the yard. As she looked at them, Lizka thought that soon they would dry out into dust and sand that she would have to clear up. She wondered where this cretin could have found so much mud in the middle of such an exceptionally hot and dry July. And what would things be like in autumn, when the rains began? And the leaves! There were always lots of leaves in autumn. Lizka remembered the rich fruit orchards of Lopukhov, which was always carpeted with a thick layer of fallen leaves when the autumn came, and she glared balefully at the maples and the men lying underneath them. One of them noticed her looking and waved to her. "Hey, what are you so angry about? So beautiful and so angry. Come on over here!"

Without answering him, Lizka quickly got up and walked away. As she walked past the large rubbish containers, she noticed that one of them was full to overflowing and the light breeze was snatching out plastic bags and pieces of paper and swirling them off across the yard.

In order to avoid curious glances or being seen accidentally by someone who knew her, at first Lizka tried to work in the mornings. She got up at four, put on her old, worn-out trainers, and with the air of a carefree jogger doing her morning run, she set out for house number 18 on the Street of the Athletes. Three hours later she arrived home, sweaty and weary, took a quick shower and usually rushed off to her classes without any time for breakfast. But after the hateful Hobgoblin caught her sleeping in a lecture and created a scandal about it, she had to abandon this approach.

Now she worked in the late evenings, when there was almost no one out and about, apart from a couple of people who lived in the building, walking their dogs. First of all Lizka went over the entire asphalted area of the yard and the pathways to all the entrances with her broom, leaving behind her several small heaps of rubbish which she later loaded into a wheelbarrow with her big shovel and took to the rubbish containers. Then she went right round the outside of the house, picking up all the empty tin cans, packaging and cellophane and putting it in a big paper sack. She found this monotonous work very calming; somehow it gave her a feeling of inner cleanliness. Lizka didn't raise her head to look at the people walking by. She watched how every stroke of the broom left the asphalt clean, free of the dirt, sand and poplar fluff that blew in from the nearby street, and she smiled at her own thoughts. She dreamed of the first time she would be paid and how she would rent a room soon. And she looked forward to buying a pair of white Yugoslavian shoes with gold buckles and nine-centimetre heels from a speculator at the flea market. She'd wear them to the discotheque and be a whole nine centimetres taller!

After two weeks the yard was transformed: thanks to Lizka's efforts the parking lot and the lawns around the house no longer resembled a rubbish dump, and her voluntary helpers, two old women pensioners, had even laid out a flower-bed in front of their entrance.

On her way to the college in the morning, Lizka made a long detour via house number 18 on the Street of the Athletes to make sure everything there was in order and no more rubbish had appeared overnight. It would have been hard for anyone to guess that this frail girl in the light dress was the yard-keeper of the house, and only the most observant person would have noticed the attentive way that she glanced round the yard.

One day her attention was caught by a plastic bag lying in the middle of the lawn in front of the house. It contained potato peelings, the head of a herring that stank repulsively and some eggshells. Lizka remembered very clearly having cleared this area the previous evening, so of course she couldn't help noticing it. Where had it come from? She looked to her left and her right: all the people hurrying about their own business paid no attention to her, only the cat dozing on a ground-floor windowsill opened one eye. Pretending that the strap of her shoe had come unfastened, she quickly bent down, carefully picked up the plastic bag with the finger and thumb of one hand and carried it to the nearest rubbish bin. All day long she was tormented by outrage at the fact that her work was not respected and anger with the people who lived in the building. She comforted herself with the thought that perhaps after all she hadn't noticed the plastic bag because the grass hadn't been cut, and so that evening she cleared the area especially thoroughly.

Next morning, however, she discovered another plastic bag in the same place, with potato peelings and empty tin cans. Lizka felt a heavy lump rising in her throat; a tremor of bitter resentment ran through her entire body and her eyes started to water. She scanned the façade of the building, hoping that she would be able to see which window the rubbish had come from, but because of the June heat almost all of them were open.

"I'll get you all the same, you swine," she said in a low voice, then picked up the bag with the cans in it and hurried off to her classes.

That Saturday evening, when she finished her work, Lizka didn't go home. Instead, she took up a position under the trees in front of the façade of the building, intending to identify the offending apartment. To her surprise, she didn't have to wait for long. An empty tin can came flying out of a third-floor window and landed silently in the grass. After quickly calculating that this window belonged to apartment number 51 on staircase number 2, Lizka went rushing inside and up the stairs.

The door was opened by a bearded man with his mouth full.

"What do you want?"

"Why do you do that?" Lizka asked, trying to make her voice sound self-assured.

"Why do I do what?" said the bearded man, stopping his chewing and goggling at her.

"Why do you throw rubbish out of the window? I work as the yard-keeper here, and I'm fed up…"

"Okay, so work away!" the fat man interrupted her rudely, and slammed the door shut.

Lizka had been entirely unprepared for such a turn of events. She stood there for a while, gazing blankly at the door like an offended child. Then she suddenly felt a desperate need to go to the toilet and she hurried down the stairs. She had to go round the left wing of the building and cut across the parking lot before she reached the bushes she needed. After pricking herself on a branch of acacia, Lizka finally squatted down behind the dense wall of bushes and thought about how in her childhood she used to dream of being a man, because they could piss standing up anywhere they liked. And also about what a loathsome character the bearded man in flat number 51 was, although secretly she was hoping that her visit would have some effect and he would stop throwing his rubbish out of the window.

But her hopes proved vain. On Monday morning the entire lawn under the windows of apartment number 51 was strewn with old newspapers, empty bottles, used toilet paper and slops of unknown origin. Beside herself with rage, Lizka completely forgot about her classes and set off to find the house manager. He listened to her carefully, but advised her not to get involved with that particular tenant. He also rang the militia to ask if they could be of any assistance, but as usual they claimed they were short of men and cars and suggested they should try to solve the problem themselves. In a fit of fury, Lizka went up to the third floor and began hammering on the bearded man's door with all her might. She clearly saw a shadow flit across the spy-hole and she knew he was watching her.

"You're nothing but a filthy swine!" Lizka shouted. "Go and pick up your own shit!"

The only reply from behind the door was a laugh and the words: "We all have our own jobs to do, and that's yours, you idiot."

A woman stuck her head out of the apartment next door and looked at Lizka indignantly.

"Stop that racket! If they don't open the door, it means there's no one home. Go away, go away immediately. You've got no reason to be here!" she hissed and disappeared again.

Lizka sat down on the steps, feeling absolutely shattered. She began crying quietly, smudging her mascara across her cheeks. Never in her life had she felt such undeserved humiliation. Despair and self-pity paralysed her thoughts and she had no idea what to do next. She pictured herself clearing up the lawn that evening in her ugly yard-keeper's coat to that bearded bastard's jeers, and suddenly she realised that no power on earth could ever force her to do it. She walked slowly outside, strode resolutely across to the repulsive garbage and picked up an empty bottle. Perhaps because there was no wind that day, or perhaps because Lizka put all of her pain, resentment and hatred into that throw, the bottle slammed precisely into the kitchen window of apartment number 51, smashed the glass and went flying inside. The confusion of tinkling glass, loud swearing and shouting that followed finally calmed Lizka down and she suddenly felt cold and empty inside. She leaned back against a maple tree and watched indifferently as tenants stuck their heads out of windows and curious passers-by gathered around her. Someone wanted to know what had happened, someone else excitedly enlightened the crowd, pointing at Lizka, someone else called the militia.

The local patrol car delivered Lizka to militia station number 9 in the Lenin District, where a smiling sergeant took her politely by the arm and ushered her into the basement, which was cold and smelled of urine. The walls were lined with the bars of the cell doors and the duty officer's desk towered above everything else on a low podium in the centre, with a stern, morose-looking captain sitting behind it.

"Ah, yet another shock worker of socialist labour?" he said with a cursory glance at Lizka.

"I'm not a prostitute," she said indignantly. "I'm a yard-keeper."

"Aha! And I'm Father Christmas," the captain laughed; then he turned to the sergeant and added: "Put her in cell number 3!"

"There aren't any seats left in there, comrade captain," protested the smiling sergeant, who was still holding Lizka by the arm.

"Well, put her in the twin cell then!"

"But there's a man in there!"

"Never mind, that won't be anything new for her."

Lizka shuddered when the cell door slammed shut behind her, and the dreadful grating of the bolt suddenly made her realise what was happening to her. Only a minute ago everything had been quite different; she had felt like a free human being, perhaps one who had done something that wasn't right, but still free, And now she was behind bars. What would happen to her studies when they found out about this in the college, and what would her mum say? Lizka was suddenly alarmed.

"Listen," she said, grabbing hold of the metal bars. "I'm not a criminal and I'm not a prostitute. I can explain everything. Let me out of here."

No one took any notice of her, so then she kicked the bars and started shouting: "Hey, do you hear me? I can't stay here! Let me out of here this instant!"

The morose captain raised his eyes.

"Listen to me carefully, my girl. I've got too much paperwork here to say this twice. The man who'll listen to what you have to say is the public prosecutor's investigator, and he'll be here tomorrow morning. The toilet here is once every four hours. No water or food. Smoking's forbidden. You have the right to one telephone call, but our telephone's been out of order since yesterday. For especially violent guests we have a gag and handcuffs. And this" – he showed her his rubber truncheon – "can have a bad effect on the functioning of your kidneys. And apart from all that, I'm in a bad mood today. Any questions?"

"Better take a seat and calm down." Lizka's cellmate sat up on the bench where he'd been lying. "You only suffer for it if you rile the cops. What's your name?"

"Lizka." She could feel her voice trembling.

"And I'm Misha," the stranger said with a smile and then, noting the fear in her eyes, he added: "Don't be afraid of me. I'm not an old lag. You could say I'm here because of a misunderstanding."

Lizka timidly sat down on the narrow bench and looked around. The floor-space in the cell was no more than three square metres and in some places the concrete walls were stained with blood that had yellowed with age. She suddenly felt so afraid that she wanted to burst into tears, but then the stranger spoke to her again: "So how old are you, then?"

"Seventeen."

"Well, then you've nothing to worry about. Juveniles aren't held responsible like other people," Misha said with a smile. "What did you do?"

Lizka told him briefly what had happened to her. And the more she said, the funnier Misha found it all. By the end of the story he was roaring with laughter, leaning back and holding his stomach in his hands. His laughter was so infectious that Lizka couldn't help starting to smile herself, and finally she started laughing too.

"You know, I even thought I saw the bottle hit him on the head," Lizka said through her laughter.

"Well, serves him right. Anyway, don't you get upset, they won't put you in jail for that kind of nonsense," Misha reassured her. "Want a smoke?"

"I'm dying for one, but how?"

Misha pulled up one trouser leg, carefully extracted one cigarette and some matches from his sock and lit up, with his hands folded protectively round the cigarette. Turning towards the wall, they handed the cigarette to each other by turn, scattering the smoke with their hands so that it wouldn't reach the nose of the morose captain. Lizka watched how greedily Misha inhaled and found herself thinking he was very handsome and she liked him. He looked about thirty-five and he wasn't very tall, but he was athletically built. The lively, smiling eyes looking out from under the curly, dark-blonde hair were bright blue.

"And why are you here?" she asked.

"Oh, that's a long story."

"Okay, we've got the whole night ahead. The investigator won't be here until morning."

"Well then, my case is a lot more complicated than yours." Misha stubbed out the cigarette against the sole of his sneaker and told his story.

THREE

MISHA WAS BORN in Ukraine, in the city of Kharkov. Until the age of eighteen he lived in tranquil serenity under the parental roof. His family was proud of his gentle manners, his school was satisfied with his progress and his friends respected him because he was always ready to help them out. He once even saved a friend's life by pulling him out of a pond when he was already half-dead and his lungs were full of water.

He had lots of interests, but the one he liked the best was music; he adored his guitar, he sang beautifully to his own playing and was never parted from it. And so when the time came for choosing a profession, he immediately took a job as an apprentice with a guitar maker, reasoning that it didn't require any specialised education and he could earn a lot of money. The industry of the USSR was churning out acoustic guitars by the hundreds of thousands, all the music shops were piled high with them; but they weren't good enough for professional musicians, and they had to go to guitar makers and pay handsomely.

Misha quickly picked up his teacher's skills; he really enjoyed studying the subtle points of the work, and soon he had his own circle of clients and he could earn a good living. He acquired a home of his own and a family and he felt grateful to fate, until it played him a dirty trick.

One day he was climbing the stairs on his way home when he saw a bunch of keys hanging in the lock of one of the other apartments. Misha shook his head dolefully at his neighbour's absentmindedness and rang the bell.

"What do you want?" asked the frightened face that appeared from behind the door.

"I'm one of your neighbours. I just wanted to tell you that you left your keys in the lock. If it had been someone else, they could have…" Before Misha could finish, strong hands grabbed him and dragged him inside. There were several men in the hallway, but he had no time to get a good look at them, because they immediately started beating him up. And when he came round there was a bloody knife in his hand, the owner of the flat was lying dead beside him and he was surrounded by militiamen and investigators.

Misha had heard about similar situations, or read about them somewhere, but of course he'd never expected to find himself caught up in one. He had a naïve belief in justice, but the Kharkov militia didn't believe in anything, they just went about piously fulfilling the plan for the number of crimes solved.

Misha's testimony was beaten out of him with the usual methods. First they wouldn't let him sleep and gave him nothing to eat or drink, then they encouraged him by applying a dumbbell to his head through the thick files of old cases, or using a brick on his kidneys, but wrapped in a felt boot so that the beatings wouldn't leave any marks. And one evening the drunken guards fastened him to the bars with handcuffs and raped him. The friend whose life he had saved, who was now a militiaman at this station, stood nearby with his eyes fixed on the ground.

Pain, fear and despair did their work, and Misha confessed to the murder. But when they finally let him out after he signed an undertaking not to leave the city, he went straight to the public prosecutor's office. Fortunately for him, there were some honest people there and they annulled his testimony and launched an internal investigation.

The public prosecutor demanded that the guilty militiamen should be convicted and punished, the militiamen claimed they were little angels and Misha hid at home, trembling like a autumn leaf.

After a while the militiamen in question came to see him, offered him a large sum of money to keep quiet and invited him to a picnic. Misha agreed, because he was also afraid of the court and he wanted to settle everything peacefully. At the picnic the militiamen apologised to him, fed him lots of kebabs and vodka, and then hanged him on the nearest pine tree.

Misha didn't remember them stringing him up. When he came round there was a young man in a tracksuit bending over him – a P.E. teacher who had happened to be running past with his class.

"What made you want to hang yourself, lad? You've got enough food and drink here for an entire platoon."

The schoolboys ate the kebabs, the teacher and Misha drank the vodka, the public prosecutor's office and the militia closed the case following the suicide of the witness and the country prepared to celebrate the sixtieth anniversary of the October Revolution.

Driven by fear, with no money or identification, Misha fled without even seeing his wife and children. Surviving on occasional earnings from odd jobs as a loader on the railway, he made his way north, to a place where no one was interested in his past and working hands were needed.

At first he helped geologists look for oil and ore, then he worked for a few years as a reindeer herder. He had always thought that the tundra was a frozen desert and no one lived there. But now he learned how colourfully it could blossom in the summer, with the fat-rumped chipmunks in the tall grass, the cunning bears and the noisy seagulls. Misha learned to castrate reindeer and eat their testicles for breakfast, to cure skins and catch fish. He was well liked by his comrades, he won their hearts with his guitar and his songs, which he wrote himself. And a man who has suffered a lot writes good songs.

One day at the campfire he heard an ancient legend that made him burst into tears. Sometimes a hunter or a fisherman would not come back home, because he might have been mauled by a bear, or perhaps been carried off into the open sea on pack ice. But if somehow he did manage to survive, he couldn't come back to his kinsmen any more. If they saw him in the distance, the tribe would take him for an evil spirit and hastily move their camp. These men were condemned to eternal solitude, and they were called the dark men. Misha thought of himself as one of those dark men.

All this time he had been thinking of nothing else but home, his warm Ukraine and his family, and so when perestroika came he had decided to go back.

On the way home he had often ended up in militia stations because he had no documents. And every time they tried to establish his identity, they had sent an enquiry to Kharkov, and the answer had always come back that this citizen had died in 1977. In most cases the militia had simply shrugged and let him go, but there was always the danger that a dishonest investigator would simply frame him for some unsolved crime and have him put him away.

Misha could have obtained new documents in the north, and any reindeer herder or geologist could have vouched for him, but he hadn't done it. He was afraid they would find him and try to kill him again, and this time they'd do the job properly.

✪

Lizka was so astounded by Misha's story that she calmed down and forgot all about her own fear. If what he'd told her was true, it must have taken a lot of courage to survive it all. She thought that in comparison with what she'd just heard, her own life could be called fortunate. Ah, if it weren't for that one incident with the bottle!

"So you haven't been home since then?" she asked.

"No. As you can see, I'm stuck here in G. and I don't know how long they're going to keep me here," Misha said with a smile.

"Tell you what, let's meet up when we get out of here."

"Okay, why not? Tell me the address, and I'll find you. I haven't anything to write it on, of course, but I'll remember it."

In the morning the investigator arrived and Lizka was taken to his office. When he started asking formal questions, like what was her name and where did she work, everything suddenly seemed very funny to her. She imagined she was a young partisan who'd been captured by the fascists and was being interrogated. For some reason she found this idea so hilarious that, although she tried hard to stop herself, she simply burst into laughter. The investigator looked up at her in astonishment.

"I don't know what you find so funny here, Ogurtsova. They put nine stitches in your victim's head."

"And what does that mean?" asked Lizka, more serious now.

"It means you won't get off with a simple fine for the window. This is article 206 of the penal code – hooliganism. So you'll be tried in court. Of course, bearing in mind that you're a juvenile and you have no record of previous misdemeanours, you're not very likely to get two years in prison. But I can guarantee you a conditional six-month sentence."

"But that's not right!" Liza exclaimed, seriously worried now.

She knew anyone with a criminal record was barred from studying in college, and they had a really hard time finding a job. And anyway, how was it possible for her, Lizka, suddenly to find herself on trial in a real court? It just couldn't happen. There had to be some way out. "What can I do? I beg you, tell me, what should I do now?"

"You should have thought about that earlier," the investigator said indifferently, handing her a pen. "Sign this and you can go. We'll summon you."

Lizka walked to the exit, past the men in militia uniform, with the most oppressive thoughts buzzing round her head. Looking in through the glass of the guardroom she saw the morose captain eating a bun with a glass of kefir. There was a man in a suit standing beside the captain, and he must have been telling him something funny, because the morose captain laughed, throwing his head back, and the kefir dribbled across his cheeks.

Once outside she began felt a bit better straight away, although she still felt like an old lag who had served five years. Nothing had happened to the world: there were cars rushing along the sun-drenched streets and people walking by, and near the park there were birds twittering. Lizka suddenly realised it was as if she was hearing them for the first time. Why had she never heard the birds before? She wanted to sit down on a bench and have a smoke, but she was swamped by a sudden, unexpected wave of alarm: no, nothing had happened to the world, but something terrible had happened to her – and she dashed to the hostel as quickly as she could.

As Lizka, weeping and wailing, told her roommates about her misadventures, she was hoping for genuine sympathy and support, but instead they lamented over her and pitied her with the kind of pity that only serves to conceal a genuine and lively curiosity. Lizka's story was inflated as rumours spread in the hostel and the college and everybody asked her the same stupid question: "What's going to happen to you now?"

The militia sent their official documents to the college and the housing department, and Hobgoblin wasted no time in excluding the student hooligan from the ranks of future medical workers. Lizka lay on her top bed in their room for days at a time, studying the cracks in the ceiling and waiting to be thrown out of her job as a yard-keeper too.

The situation was saved, as usual, by Nina's decisive action. Through some friends of friends she found a lawyer and took advice from him. Then she got everyone on their floor to sign a statement that they would take collective responsibility for Lizka as a group, and she made the supervisor of the hostel sign it too. After that, she went to the director of the housing department and asked him not to sack Lizka, promising him there wouldn't be a trial. And finally, she went to the victim to persuade him to withdraw the complaint he had made to the militia.

She came back home late in the evening, tired but smiling.

"Well, what happened?" asked Lizka, jumping down off her bed.

"You have to know how to talk to people. You'll be glad to know he's withdrawn his complaint. You owe me," Nina said with a wink.

"What did you do, sleep with him?" Vika and Olga asked in a single voice.

"Are you crazy! I just told him that if my friend ended up in the dock I'd smash him over the head in the entryway some time. And not with a bottle, with a hammer."

"Thank you, Nina," said Lizka, and tears sprang to her eyes.

"Fine words butter no parsnips. You owe me your sausage coupons. And right now it's time for everyone to sleep."

"What a strong, self-confident girl she is," Lizka thought to herself. This was the third night Lizka hadn't been able to sleep because of the events of recent days. "Nina's like an icebreaker that breaks straight through any obstacle and always wins out." Lizka wanted very much wanted to be like her.

The next day, when Lizka was at home alone, looking through the advertisements in the newspapers in the hope of finding a new place to study, Misha suddenly appeared in the doorway. He smelled of vodka and he was holding a bouquet of wild flowers.

"Hello, Liza," he said, holding out the bouquet to her.

Lizka blushed for a moment, because no one ever called her "Liza" and also because Misha had spoken those two words in a very affectionate way, but she immediately took a grip on herself and offered him a chair.

"Well, how are things? Sit down and tell me."

"Things aren't exactly great, of course. I've got no money and no place to live, but the main thing is that I'm free again." Misha smiled. "The answer came back from Kharkov again that I died a long time ago. You know, it reminds me of that man Petukhov in the film, the one who asked the polyclinic for a doctor's cert that he was alive. Roman law – a man without a document simply doesn't exist. But I'll think of something. After all, I have a good trade to fall back on. Anyway, I'll just have to hang about in this town for a while. Ah, by the way, is there a guitar here?"

"I think they had one in one of the rooms."

"Do you think you could get it? And meanwhile I'll organise some tea." Misha smiled his enchanting smile again and stuck the electric element into the kettle as if he was at home.

While Lizka went to get the guitar she had time to think about many things, and she didn't even go straight back into her room, but stood outside the door for a while. Her own troubles seemed quite childish now. And how hard it must be for Misha just now. She pitied him and wanted to help him, only she didn't know how. And apart from that, she was very glad that he had come. Sweet Misha was a little naïve, but he was courageous; he had a power of attraction that she didn't want to resist.

As they drank the tea, to which Misha added vodka from the half-empty bottle that he'd brought with him, he suddenly said: "Listen, why don't you come to the Crimea with me? What do you want to study in G. for anyway? I'll give you sunshine, palm trees and the Black Sea."

"You're just drunk," Lizka said with a laugh.

"So what? The two of us will give concerts and earn heaps of money. Do you have a good ear?"

"I don't know."

"Well, sing something."

"What?"

"Anything, it doesn't matter, don't be shy."

Lizka kept saying no at first, but then she closed her eyes, collected herself and sang her favourite four lines.

"Magnificent! You've got talent. Surely you don't want to be a cook or a weaver, not with a voice like that?"

"You're just talking nonsense," Lizka retorted, but in her heart she felt glad.

"Now I'll have a go," said Misha. He picked up the guitar, tuned it quickly and started to sing.

Lizka had never heard anything more beautiful than Misha's songs. He sang one after another without stopping and Lizka felt like crying when she remembered her mother and the orchards in Lopukhov, or she smiled and tapped her foot in time with the lively tune. Misha kept playing, making occasional pauses to give his mug some attention, and Lizka listened to him, following the movements of his lips and hands, and she realised that she'd fallen in love.

They sat there until the evening.

"Listen, why don't you stay a bit longer? My roommates will be back soon."

On the one hand Lizka wanted the other girls to enjoy Misha's musical skill as well, but on the other hand, she was already feeling jealous.

"No, it's time for me to go."

"But where are you going to spend the night?"

"Don't worry about me, I'm well used to it." Misha began getting ready to go. "Listen, you couldn't lend me a bit of money, could you?"

"Of course," said Lizka, taking her wallet out of the drawer of her bedside locker. "Here, there's only a twenty. It's the last I have, but I get paid tomorrow, so take it."

"It's nice to be paid." Misha drank the remains of the vodka and kissed Lizka on the cheek. "Maybe you could take me out somewhere tomorrow?"

"I'd love to."

When Nina came back from work Vika and Olga, who had got back an hour earlier, just couldn't wait to tell her that Lizka had found herself an admirer. They showed her the flowers and the empty bottle and told her the room had smelled of a man.

"You didn't waste any time!" said Nina, looking at Lizka suspiciously. "When did you manage that? But it's your future you should be thinking about now, not boys."

All that evening the girls made fun of Lizka and showered her with questions, but she just smiled mysteriously and said nothing. She was happy.

The fact that Misha was almost twice her age didn't bother Lizka at all. On the contrary, she was happy to take on the role of the apprentice and tried to imitate everything he did. He had won her heart with his sharp wit and the way he could just shrug off difficulties. Misha was different from all the men she'd met so far. He was so gentle and affectionate with her that after their first night together her aversion to sex disappeared for ever.

They met almost every evening somewhere in the city, and on Saturdays, when Nina worked the night shift and Vika and Olga went back to their parents in the country, Misha stayed overnight in the hostel.

Lizka wanted to know a bit more about the man she loved: what he did during all those days, where he slept and where he got the money to live on, but he avoided the subject and only spoke about his plans for the future. He would try to persuade Lizka to hitchhike to Ukraine with him, and then reject that idea because he didn't have any documents, or he would say he was planning to open a guitar repair workshop to earn some money for the journey. And while he was painting a rainbow-coloured picture of a carefree life beside a warm sea, Lizka was spending half of her pay as a yard-keeper on him. With her first wages she bought him a few clothes, since he was pretty down-at-heel, and he suggested blowing her next pay packet in a restaurant. She had to choose between the Yugoslavian shoes and the restaurant, and she chose the restaurant, because she'd never been in one.

When he arrived at the hostel at the agreed time, Misha barely recognised her. As usual, she had borrowed a new blouse and a few bits of imported make-up from her roommates and she looked magnificent, positively radiating charm and joy.

"There's ninety roubles here," she said, handing Misha the money. "Where shall we go?"

"I'm afraid that might only be enough for one," Misha said with a naïve expression. "Couldn't you borrow some from someone?"

"I know Nina has a bit of money in her locker, but she's still on duty."

"That's no problem, I got a good order for a guitar and I'll be able to pay it back in just a couple of days, literally."

"Seriously?"

"Word of honour."

"Perhaps we should wait for Nina?" Lizka didn't want to take the money without asking.

"Don't be silly, we're always waiting for something or other. We can't enjoy life because all the time we have the feeling that there's something we have to do first and then afterwards we can live without worrying. When is this afterwards? When we die? So we can live without worrying, we're always trying to jump some barrier: get a good apartment, earn a lot of money, buy this or that. But jumping barriers is just life, and we have to live right now, every day. Do you understand?"

"I think so," said Lizka. She took fifty roubles out of Nina's purse and snuggled in under Misha's arm. "Let's go."

Just at that moment Nina entered the room, and when she saw Misha, her face dropped.

"Semyon?" Nina's eyes narrowed and her cheeks flushed.

"Who's Semyon?" asked Lizka, blinking in confusion.

"What are you doing here, you bastard?" Nina grabbed the first thing that came to hand – a cast-iron frying pan – and went straight for Misha.

"Nina, please! Liza, I can explain everything!" Misha exclaimed, then he flung himself sideways, pushed Nina out of the way and skipped out of the door.

"Stop, you louse!" Nina shouted and went dashing after him.

They rushed along the entire length of the corridor and ended up on the landing, where Misha jumped up on to the banister and slid downstairs at high speed.

"And don't let me see you here again!" Nina shouted after him in a hoarse, breathless voice.

"What happened?" Lizka asked in fright when Nina arrived back in the room, panting and clutching the frying pan. "Do you know Misha?"

"He's not Misha, he's Semyon. How did he get here?"

"Semyon? I don't understand, Nina, why do you call him Semyon?"

"Because that's the crook's name. About three years ago one of my friends ended up on his long list of victims. By the way, check to see if your money's still there."

"I…we were going to go to a restaurant, I gave it all to him. And I borrowed a bit from you too…"

"What? So that's your friend?" Nina started laughing hysterically. "Well, you're a real fool, Lizka. Semyon's a lousy con-man, and an alcoholic and a desperate gambler. I used to see him around quite a lot, but then they say he went somewhere up north to escape from his card debts. His usual line is comforting rich widows, but he must be in a really bad way if he's latched on to you."

"Why are people so mean and cruel? What are you doing to me, people?" Lizka thrust her face into her pillow and burst into tears.

FOUR

AUTUMN SET IN abruptly: sharp north winds brought a sudden chill and tore the yellow leaves off the trees, the shroud of grey clouds was only occasionally pierced by pale rays of sunshine, the rain lashed down incessantly and people walked about in a state of deep depression.

Large puddles had formed in the yard of number 18, Street of the Athletes, and Lizka had extra work to do now. At first she swept the rubbish and the leaves mixed with sawdust into the puddles, and when they had soaked up the water, she carried the liquid filth to the container in her yard-keeper's barrow. Since it was starting to get dark earlier and get light later, but the street lighting had not yet been switched on for reasons of economy, Lizka had to work during the afternoon. But at least now she could luxuriate in bed until almost lunchtime.

She woke up with everyone else at the loud trilling of the alarm-clock and watched from her second-storey perch as her roommates got up. Nina was always the first to jump out of bed. She occupied the shower and splashed about in it, singing some uplifting tune. Where did she get all that energy and enthusiasm?

"When you sing, you give the impression of not having a problem in the world," Lizka said to Nina as she was getting dressed.

"I've got problems way over my head," Nina answered with a

laugh. "My architect's granny just refuses to die. She's eighty-nine already! Why can't she give the young generation a chance to live a bit? It's a seditious thought, of course, but if we could move into her apartment, we'd get married straight away. And anyway, you have to keep up and on the go all the time to avoid falling into a melancholy stupor. And you have to think less!"

And while Vika and Olga were still rubbing their eyes and plodding off to the shower with sour faces, Nina was already brewing tea and making sandwiches.

Think less. No, Lizka couldn't help thinking now, and she had plenty to think about. Her studies had come to nothing, she'd fallen in love with a swindler, she was living in a hostel in the workers' quarter with three roommates who were basically just like her, girls with no real prospects. But life gave other people somewhere else a great love, a prosperous life and happiness. It was all very unfair. And who decided these things? Who divided people into those who were content with life and those who weren't? Perhaps everything depended on her and no one else? In that case she had to do something. Study, work or find a husband – someone kind and handsome. No, better someone rich, even if he wasn't very kind or very handsome.

Lizka looked at Vika and Olga, who were getting ready to have breakfast.

Take them, for instance. They'd be good nurses, they'd get married, they'd have children. But what was so good about that? They'd also have to go running round the shops with heavy bags and spend half their lives in queues. They and their men would put money away for a car and in ten years they'd scrape together enough for a Lada. And that would be their lives! Was that what they called a worthy future? And if the future was old age, then why did they force us to think about it from the moment we were born? Maybe she shouldn't do anything after all. Simply drift with the current, be content to work as a yard-keeper. After all, someone had to sweep the streets. But then her life would be a dead end, like her mother's. Her mother was in a dead end because she didn't have youth, or beauty, or a goal. And what goal did Lizka have? To change everything for the better. To send her lousy fate to hell and change everything before it was too late.

Lizka jumped down from her bed to give the girls a goodbye kiss on the cheek and close the door after them. Then she made herself a huge sausage sandwich, picked up a novel off the shelf and lay down again.

Lizka had not read much or very often in her life, but now, either because she had nothing to do, or because she was trying to find some answers to her questions in the books, she had become an enthusiastic reader of novels. Love novels, historical novels, crime novels, adventure novels – they all absorbed her completely, transporting her to a world that was different and fascinating, but they didn't contain any guidelines for action or any answer to the most important question of all – how to carry on living her life. The main characters in these novels were never short of money, their mothers didn't send them potatoes, jam and a little bit of cash from Lopukhov. They fought courageously, loved passionately, did things that were absolutely wild and crazy and no one ever punished them for it. They didn't know anything about empty shop shelves, Leninist working Saturdays and compulsory annual training in civil defence. They weren't real people like Lizka, they were just characters, only invented to live for the few days it took her to read a book.

But in almost all the novels there was a central character who either defeated his enemies and overcame difficulties, or solved

crimes, or protected the weak and oppressed, or performed feats
of heroism in the name of his beloved. Honest, intelligent, noble,
without any accommodation or financial problems, sometimes with
bad habits, but never ill; sensitive, considerate, affectionate and, of
course, young and handsome. Where was he, Lizka's prince on a
white horse?

Lizka didn't go looking for her prince on her own, she went with
Nina, because she knew her way around the city and she had friends
who were former patients in several cafés and discotheques. Both
girls dolled themselves up as impressively as they could, without
sparing the imported make-up that was so incredibly expensive,
and counted up their roubles. Since they only had enough money
for coffee and ice-cream, the plan of action dictated itself: occupy
an empty table, make lively conversation with each other and laugh
loudly, pretending that they weren't interested in men.

"Our mini-skirts, the cognac and the rock-and-roll will do the
rest," Nina said knowingly. "If the nets are set correctly it won't be
long before something gets caught. At least we won't be leaving with
empty stomachs. And don't forget to walk the way I taught you –
move your legs from the hips."

They walked round the night-time city for a long time, shivering
from the cold. Here and there the puddles were already beginning to
freeze over and they glinted dismally in the moonlight; occasional
taxis went rushing past them and on the corner an insatiable tom
had driven a cat up a tree.

"Maybe we could try here?" said Lizka, pointing to a house
of culture with a sign that said "Sputnik". "My teeth are already
chattering out here."

"No way. Only kids come here. And only the girls dance, while
the lanky young brutes sit on the benches round the walls and

never show any initiative." Nina dragged Lizka further along the street.

They didn't go into the next house of culture either – according to Nina, only people who were over thirty went there – or into the third one, where you were unlikely to find anyone except ex-convicts. They stopped outside the restaurant "Rossiya". The haughty doorman scanned them with a critical glance, but he didn't say anything and let them in.

Inside it was noisy and smoky and all the tables were taken, apart from one in the corner with a "Reserved" sign on it. Without saying a word, Nina dragged Lizka after her and set off with a determined stride towards that very table.

"Sit down!"

"What are you doing? They'll throw us out straight away." Lizka glanced round in fright at the waiter coming towards them.

"I beg your pardon," he said, with an expression of extreme indignation on his face. "This table's taken."

"Hello, Vadik," said Nina, turning towards him with a smile. "Don't you remember me?"

"I'm sorry, I can't recall. Please leave this table!"

"Ah, but would you believe it – ever since you came to our clinic I just can't get the sight of those sores of yours out of my mind."

"No so loud, please!" The waiter turned pale and his eyes acquired a shifty look.

"Bring us two chocolate cocktails, you halfwit," Nina said and smiled again. "Please."

"Just a moment," the waiter said in a metallic-sounding voice and withdrew in embarrassment, taking the "Reserved" sign with him.

They sat there for a few more minutes, and then Lizka felt someone looking at her. Glancing round, she saw two young men sitting at the next table, one of whom was staring hard at her legs. He noticed her glance, but he didn't turn away as anybody else might have done in a similar situation, he just carried on devouring her with his eyes.

"Do you know who these two are?" Lizka asked Nina, indicating the men she meant with a nod of her head.

"Forget it! They're out of our league," Nina said casually. "The one who's eying you up is Victor Mikhailovich, secretary of the Municipal Communist Youth League Committee, and the one beside him is a journalist from the *Agitator's Sputnik*. I've forgotten what he's called."

The Komsomol secretary carried on ogling Lizka without wavering, and she didn't know what to do. To smile at him would be too forward, and so she decided to look him over as well. Skinny, with hunched shoulders, a Greek nose and thin, straight lips set in a permanent smirk – she didn't like him. But she was attracted by his eyes – they were brazen and masterful, piercing and domineering. She couldn't keep up her stare and she turned away in embarrassment. Then he slowly got up, came towards them equally slowly, but confidently, and leaned towards them a little, and both of them caught a whiff of expensive eau-de-cologne.

"Good evening, ladies. Would you care to join us?" the soft velvety voice asked, but it sounded like an order, and even the glib and perky Nina could find no answer, subdued by the magic of its power.

"You need to relax," the secretary said when they were seated at his table, and he poured cognac for everybody.

The journalist was already very tipsy and therefore talkative. He proposed a toast to their meeting, although in fact nobody had actually introduced anybody to anybody else. The secretary never took his eyes off Lizka and he said nothing, leaving it up to his comrade to conduct the conversation. Nina answered his questions and asked a few of her own. She lied and said they were students at the Technical Institute.

But Lizka felt uncomfortable under that cynical and somehow bestial gaze and so she hit the drink hard. Soon everything started swimming round inside her head: meaningless phrases, a roast duck, red, laughing, drunken faces veiled by tobacco smoke, music and strong, muscly hands on her waist while she was dancing. She talked all sorts of nonsense, she laughed, she broke the heel of one of her shoes – the ones that Nina had given her. Afterwards, Lizka was sick in the toilet, Nina and the journalist disappeared somewhere, then she was alone with the secretary, and then he was carrying her somewhere over his shoulder, walking upstairs.

"Give me more Armenian cognac! Give me a glass!" she shouted. "Don't throw your rubbish out of the windows! Hurrah for Armenian cognac! Long live the sunny Caucasus!"

When she found herself in somebody else's huge bed the next morning, Lizka realised that no one had slept with her. On the small table beside the bed there was a glass of apple juice, and underneath it she saw a note: "Good morning, Liza. If you want to go, just close the door on your way out. If you want to stay, there are rice croquettes in the fridge. I'll be back at four. Victor." Lizka wrapped herself in the man's towelling dressing-gown that a considerate hand had hung over the back of a chair, beside her own carefully folded clothes. Then she stretched twice, so hard that something cracked somewhere, yawned and began looking round the apartment.

First of all she was amazed by the size of Victor's home. There were five rooms here, and Lizka found a staircase in one of them. Overcome by curiosity, she quickly climbed the steps and found another two rooms upstairs. Knowing perfectly well that apartments like this couldn't exist in her country, Lizka dashed across to the balcony to find out exactly where she was. The house she was in was identical with the five-storey Khrushchev-period buildings that were standing to the right and the left of it, and that completely threw her. But just at that moment the first snowflake fell on Lizka's nose, bringing with it a simple solution to her puzzle. Victor must have taken out the dividing wall between two standard apartments and then added on one more from the next floor up. For a brief moment Lizka was enraged: she had to make do with a bed standing on top of another one in twenty square metres shared with three roommates, while this bourgeois swine was calmly occupying three apartments on his own! But this feeling of injustice was immediately replaced by a different thought. A prince had to have a castle. And if Victor was her prince, he was a real one, with a real castle. Lizka carried on wandering round the rooms, and her amazement just kept on growing. There was very little furniture: instead of the usual tables, cupboards and chairs, there were low shelves on the lacquered wooden floor, with all sorts of things standing on them: intricate seashells, lots of stones of every possible colour and size, little figurines of wood or clay that represented African or Indian gods, copper amulets and other exotic bits and pieces. There were paintings without any frames hanging on the walls, but no matter how hard Lizka tried, she just couldn't work out what they were pictures of. But the thing that astonished her most of all was the room with the birch trees. It was completely empty apart from five or six genuine birch trees, fixed between the floor and the ceiling and covered with transparent lacquer. The paper covering the wall behind them was a photograph showing the edge of a forest and several peasant huts against a background of boundless open countryside.

And standing in front of the trees there was a large armchair and an imported cassette-deck. Liza immediately wanted to listen to the cassette, but after glancing at the keys with the non-Russian letters on them, she decided not to try, because she wasn't much good with foreign languages.

Lizka lingered a bit longer in another room, which was probably the study where he worked, in order to study the contents of the desk. As well as a huge number of documents, which Lizka looked through without understanding a thing, she found Victor's passport: twenty-eight and not married! The walls of the study were decorated with various certificates, diplomas and formal expressions of thanks, which testified that their owner was a great party activist, an outstanding student and a first-class marksman. Red delegate's credentials indicated that Victor had taken part in all sorts of conventions and conferences that had been held in Moscow, Sochi and Yalta. Well then, she could already be proud of her prince even now. Of course, he could have been a little more handsome, with a better figure. But who could be choosy about princes? You simply waited for them, and when they came there was no point in thinking about anything. The main thing was that he was intelligent and rich, exactly what she'd wanted.

Liza also noticed a special smell that hung in the air here. She couldn't even have tried to guess where it was coming from. It could have been a good eau-de-toilette, or the lacquer on the parquet, but it carried a hint of freshness, cleanliness and comfort; it was calming and relaxing. She wouldn't have liked to go back to her slum in the workers' quarter for anything in the world now.

"What an interesting and unusual character this Victor is, after all," Lizka thought, and then she remembered the croquettes and set off for the kitchen.

✪

Victor Mikhailovich really was an exceptional man, who had already managed to make a successful career for himself, despite his young age. He had developed a keen interest in Komsomol activities when he was still at school, and after he graduated from the philosophical faculty in the university of G. they had completely taken over his life. First of all, not without a certain amount of help from his father, a deputy minister of heavy industry, he had been made the head of the ideology and politics sector in one of the district committees of the Communist Party, and a year after that he was already the second secretary of the municipal party committee, thanks in large degree to his skills as an orator. Victor Mikhailovich was able to speak about everything and nothing at the same time, he always had a couple of hundred aphorisms and catchphrases ready and waiting, he quoted Marx, Engels and Brezhnev frequently and relevantly and he always emerged victorious from any dispute. People were spellbound when they listened to him, they nodded their heads, they might laugh or even burst into tears under the impression made by his words and, as a rule, after ten minutes they were primed and ready for whatever action he was inciting them to carry out. His power of persuasion was so great that Cicero, Lenin and Hitler could have envied him. The upper levels of the party valued him for this, the lower levels drank in every word he uttered in respectful awe. Even the first secretary of the municipal committee, whose speeches were written by Victor Mikhailovich, was a little afraid of him.

Before perestroika Victor Mikhailovich's work, apart from paperwork and red tape, had basically consisted of meetings with labour collectives, students and school pupils, at which he spoke passionately about socialist construction and the Komsomol's role in it and appealed to everyone to join the ranks of this glorious

organisation. When Gorbachev's winds of change had begun to
blow, bringing cost accounting and the first co-operatives, he had
adjusted his orientation a little. He had replaced the red cloth on
the presidium's table with a green one, removed the large wooden
rostrum with the carafe and abolished the compulsory singing of "I
shall never leave the Komsomol, I shall be young for ever!" before
every Komsomol meeting.

"Comrades!" he would begin, addressing his listeners in a
dramatic voice, sitting erect on his chair after the new democratic
fashion. "Let us have no more demagogy and formalism! We need
concrete work! We have not been giving any attention at all to finding
Komsomol members jobs and providing for their recreation!"

And so, under his leadership, there soon appeared Komsomol
construction companies erecting elite homes in the dormitory areas
of the city, Komsomol shops, Komsomol videobars and a Komsomol
casino. This economic activity earned Victor Mikhailovich a
substantial income and did not conflict in any way with the work he
loved so much in the party hierarchy. His long-term goal was a party
leader's post at the regional level and he was preparing for entry to
the Higher Party School.

Lizka suddenly came to her senses. She had got so carried away with
inspecting the flat and reading the books that she hadn't noticed
the time flying by. Since she hadn't gone to work, she could at least
cook something. After a glance into the cupboard and the fridge,
she decided on spaghetti and mince. At a quarter to four she was
dashing backwards and forwards between the spaghetti that kept
trying to jump out of the saucepan and the mirror, because her hair
was being awkward and refused to stay as she arranged it. She had
just straightened the cushion on the divan in the drawing-room and

put a book back on the shelf when the lock on the door clicked and Victor appeared.

"So you know how to cook. That's good," he said in a rather cool voice, but all in all it was clear that he was glad to see her.

"You have a big apartment," said Lizka, trying to smile.

She stood there in front of him, shifting from one foot to the other, without the slightest idea of how she ought to behave. Victor seemed to understand this and he took her by the hand and led her into the kitchen.

"Let's eat. I had a bottle of good Moldavian wine here some-where."

At the table Lizka watched and envied Victor's skill with a fork and spoon, cursing herself for cooking this particular dish. She never used her spoon and because she was nervous her fork was behaving so clumsily that she had to lean down low over her plate. She sucked in the strings of spaghetti one at a time, glancing at Victor from under her eyebrows and expecting him to tell her off, and she felt absolutely terrible.

"How are you getting on in the institute?" he asked suddenly, and Lizka almost choked.

Oh, that Nina with that stupid story of hers! Lizka reached for her glass, thinking over her answer. If she wanted the relationship to continue, what point was there in lying?

"I'm not a student. My friend made that up, to make us seem more respectable. I'm a yard-keeper."

"Well? Do you enjoy it?" Victor's face didn't betray a single emotion.

Lizka suddenly felt like shouting at him and telling him to stop mocking her. Couldn't he see the way she was dressed, how awkward she felt with him, that his imperturbable air was depressing her? But instead of that she said: "Yes, I enjoy it. Lots of fresh air and flexible working hours."

"Don't lie to me the next time," Victor said in a warmer voice. "All right?"

"All right."

Then he suddenly jumped up, dashed at Lizka and pressed his lips passionately against hers. The table began to shake, the salt cellar fell on the floor and broke. Lizka mumbled something, but he was already dragging her towards the divan. Clothes went flying in all directions, a plush teddy-bear stuck its plastic nose painfully into Lizka's shoulder blade, buttons skeetered across the parquet floor and Lizka began feeling sorry for her best blouse. "It's just like in a film," were the last words that ran through her head before his bony fingers reached the spot at which Lizka's thoughts ended.

The second secretary knew what he was doing when he made love, but he was in too much of a rush and a bit egocentric. If Lizka had chosen to compare Victor Mikhailovich and Misha or, rather, Semyon, then she would have preferred the latter. Why was it that all the really good men were bastards?

Victor offered her a cigarette and lit up himself.

"You know, I think I ought to be honest with you, because I'd like the same thing from you. I can't call the feeling that I get when I look at you love, but I'm just consumed with desire when I look at your legs and your backside. And apart from that, I want to have a woman beside me who can help me."

"What? Don't you have anyone to wash your socks?" said Lizka, trying to joke, and she wrapped her legs round Victor's body, but he was very serious.

"I don't mean a wife. I take my washing to the laundry and I usually only eat at home at the weekends. And I think it's unlikely

I could put up with the shared concerns of family life and children and, worst of all, my wife's relatives. I need a woman as a secure back-up. You've probably guessed that I have a difficult job that means I always have to be in the public eye, demonstrating my strength and winning our men's games. Our competitors in the informal economic associations that have multiplied like cockroaches thanks to perestroika are just waiting for us to stumble and expose some weak spot to them. This so-called openness makes it harder and harder to manage the organisation. I require a lot of courage and strength right now. You can't imagine how hard it is always being strong. That's why the top priority task of the moment is reinforcing the inner defences. You can give me a woman's tenderness, sympathy and understanding – all the things my mother once used to give me. Don't worry, you won't have to do anything, just be there beside me, that's all. It's a bit like a deal, really. Do you understand me?"

"Yes," Lizka replied, although she wasn't listening at all because of the thought nagging at her mind: was he was going to make love to her again and again? She hadn't cooled off yet, she wanted more sex.

"And it's an honest deal," Victor continued. "You get something in return. You won't need to worry about your material welfare. You won't be obliged to work, although I would advise you to do something with yourself, and start by studying. I don't intend to treat you as a thing, quite the opposite; I'll try my best to help you develop. I'm good at that. You're my ninth girlfriend."

Those words made Lizka start and she felt an unfamiliar, sharp pricking of resentment somewhere inside, but she was quick to reassure herself: after all, he was older and more experienced than her.

"How do you mean 'try your best to help me develop'?" she asked.

"For a start we'll get you some clothes. Then I'll give you some helpful books and introduce you to some intelligent people. Of course, I have to confess that I don't intend to help you in your career. In fact, it annoys me if a woman is more successful than I am. And I'm afraid of getting too used to women, because the inevitable parting might rob me of my strength for a while. You see, I'm being frank with you. Feeding bullshit to my herd of young comrades sometimes makes me feel so tired that I don't feel like lying at home as well. Perhaps you're still too young and foolish to understand all this, but those are two qualities I've come to value in others in the course of my professional activity."

Lizka felt she'd been insulted, but she didn't understand how. And while she was wondering if she ought to put on an offended expression, Victor seemed to read her thoughts.

"Don't be offended. It's wonderful to be young and foolish. As people get older, they don't get any wiser, they just get shrewder and more cynical and change their masks more often. And the final condition: you have to join the Komsomol. Imagine what my enemies would say if they found out I was living with an ideologically immature Soviet citizen."

"And what do I have to do for that?"

"With me, nothing. Bring me two photographs and the next day I'll give you your Komsomol card. If you agree with everything, we can move your things in tomorrow." Victor pointed to a hook with the keys to the apartment hanging on it. "Those are for you."

All the next week Lizka was almost happy as she rushed round the city dealing with pleasant problems. She left her job at the housing department with no regrets and at the same time she joined the Komsomol and happily signed out of the hostel. She said goodbye to her friends, sitting on her two suitcases from Lopukhov that were already packed, with a mug of diluted medical spirit in her hand.

"Some people are lucky," Vika said enviously.

"She was only pretending to be a quiet one, just look what a big fish she's landed," Olga laughed.

"And what's that to you, you damn lesbos? You haven't got a clue about what can be done with men," Nina interrupted, then she turned to Liska and added: "We still don't know how things will work out between you and this Komsomol big-shot, but you know you have a place to come back to if you need to. We won't let any new lodgers in. And in general, if you need help, get in touch!"

"Wonderful, kind Nina, thank you," said Lizka and threw her arms round Nina's neck. "I won't forget you, I'll come to see you."

"That's not likely!" Nina chuckled. "I know your Victor Mikhailovich's kind. He's a standard tyrant, a dictator and a real pain. He won't allow it."

"I'll come to see you anyway; he won't find out."

"Goodbye!"

"Goodbye!"

Tears sprang to the girls' eyes and they all hugged and kissed each other.

As she walked towards the exit along the decrepit corridor that smelled of urine, Lizka remembered what Nina had said about Vika and Olga being lesbians. It explained a lot. Lizka had always wondered why the two of them went everywhere together and they had no boyfriends. This was a subject that had bothered Lizka when she was still at school, forcing her to look inside herself and answer the question of why she was attracted by the naked bodies of the girls in her class and secretly looked at them in the changing-room. But she didn't want to think too much about that right now; she had so many new things to look forward to.

In the two years that Lizka lived with Victor Mikhailovich she learned a great deal and began to look at certain things in a different way. At the beginning she could sense the barbed, mocking comments behind her back and the offensive, condescending attitude of Victor's friends and former girlfriends towards her, but she gradually merged into his social circle and settled down. She took a course and qualified as a typist, and thanks to her connections she got a job as a secretary in the instructors' section of the municipal party committee. Lizka typed slowly and made mistakes, but as Victor Mikhailovich's girlfriend, she was by no means overloaded with work and the rest of the time she carried on reading romantic novels. But when Victor found her reading one day, he created such a furious a scene about it that afterwards the orthographical dictionary became the most important book on her desk.

"Just look at that dress she's wearing!" Victor's previous girlfriend, Alla, who also worked there, said, laughing at her. "You must have bought it at the flea market!"

"Take a look at yourself, you cow!" Lizka answered her back and immediately felt better.

When he occasionally witnessed these squabbles, Victor only laughed. He took a very caring attitude towards Lizka, trying to educate her and foster her development. No one ever contradicted Alla and she hadn't expected such cheek from Lizka, so she just stood there, batting her eyelashes. Victor was highly amused by this reaction and he said affectionately to Lizka: "That dress really is a bit too bright and colourful. Let's go to the sewing shop together this evening."

Lizka's indignation at the hypocrisy of the Komsomol leaders, which used to offend her to the depths of her soul, also subsided, and she enjoyed exploiting her position. The doors of all the elite shops and even one foreign currency shop were open to her, and at the back doors of other shops she could buy unlimited quantities of food products that were in short supply, the ones other people stood in kilometre-long queues to get.

"Do you see those insects crawling about?" Victor would say to her, standing on the balcony with a cigarette in his hand and pointing down at the people hurrying on their way to work. "They're not the masters of life. They work to support their life, but they don't create it, as I and my friends do. They're not even aware of the meaninglessness of their own existence and they believe blindly in our propaganda nonsense. Do you think they need salami and bananas? No. Hoping for something better is enough for them. That's enough to satisfy them. And how seriously they take the rules of this meaningless, exploitative game foisted on them from above, how inspired they are! Sometimes I don't know what I want to do most – simply burst out laughing or puke on them from up here."

Victor treated Lizka to monologues like this one almost every day, and sometimes he took her to his parties, where people had strange conversations that frightened her, and they discussed books that were banned in the USSR. Lizka tried to stop going to these gatherings, but Victor was adamant.

"Are you going to see your collective farm girls in the hostel again?" he would ask.

"They're not collective farm girls!" Lizka would reply, defending her friends.

"That's not important. They have a bad influence on you!"

"But I'm bored with your friends, and I'm bored sitting at home with nothing to do!"

"That's just it, you're not doing anything! What about some studying? Are you going to go to college at all?"

"There's still a year to go until the entrance exams."

"But you have to prepare for them in advance."

Although Lizka realised that Victor was right, her head was filled with thoughts of an entirely different kind. In Victor's circle there were too many rules of etiquette, too much insincerity, too many mealy-mouthed conversations and counterfeit feelings. Lizka had a yen for something a bit simpler, the company of people like herself, people she would understand.

"Let's go to the discotheque," she suggested.

"If you just want to wiggle your backside about, then let's go to the gym or the pool."

Lizka could never have said that she loved Victor, but she respected him and felt grateful to him. She had really become attached to him, as the father she had never had, or as a teacher, but more and more often she found herself looking at younger and more attractive men. And Victor could tell. And in addition, the envious Alla had told him that Lizka flirted with men who visited their department and accepted chocolates from them. The trauma he had suffered in his youth when the woman he loved betrayed him had destroyed for ever his belief that a woman could be faithful to one man for all her life. Instead of his former tenderness, mutual understanding and moral support, more and more often he tried to humiliate her and he revelled in his own superiority. Whatever she said, it irritated him unbearably. He would contradict her tactfully, with superficial politeness, but in a way that made Lizka afraid to express her own opinion. And when he did it in front of people they knew, she felt like hiding away in another room and crying. Their relationship was developing cracks.

FIVE

BABBLING BROOKS, SQUAWLING cats and avitaminosis announced the arrival of spring. Lizka's young blood began to froth, her heart was filled with a vague and pleasant agitation and the ginger-haired, freckle-faced Tatar Artur appeared on the horizon of her life. For some reason Lizka had always liked Tatars. She thought they were the friendliest and most good-hearted people in Russia, always prepared to help, and they appreciated humour.

Lizka fell in love with this muscular, well-built young man's freckles at first sight, the moment he appeared in the doorway of the municipal committee's reception.

"Can I help you?" asked Lizka. She couldn't help smiling as she repeated the well-worn phrase.

"Yes. I want to leave the Komsomol, but I don't know who to hand my card in to. And I'm also looking for a wife. You wouldn't happen to be single, would you?"

"Slow down, handsome," Liza laughed and showed him which door he needed.

Shortly after Artur went in through the door, she heard loud shouting and abuse from behind it, but when he came back out, his face was beaming.

"Well now, that's one job done!" he said, rubbing his hands

together and looked at Lizka. "Would you like to have lunch with me?"

"Are you always this fast?"

"Almost always."

Although Lizka still had another two pages to type, she didn't want to let such a little cutie get away.

"Why not? Let's go."

She was genuinely surprised that Artur had parted with his Komsomol card so simply. Although it wasn't publicly acknowledged, Komsomol members enjoyed certain privileges when it came to getting a place in an educational institute or promotion at work.

"Why? Do you begrudge the money for the membership dues?" she asked, adopting the tone of his own playful behaviour.

"The damned Komsomol can go to hell!" said Artur with a wave of his hand. "Do this, do that. Who do they think they are to be giving instructions? Always interfering in industry and agriculture, as if they understood anything about them!"

They walked out of the municipal committee building and set off towards the cafeteria on the opposite side of the street.

"And why are you so angry with them?"

Over lunch Artur told her that he worked as a trolleybus driver, and because of the black ice last week he'd dented someone's rear bumper. After investigation by the traffic police and the management of the trolleybus office, which had made him recompense the driver of the damaged car out of his own pay, the final straw had been the public reprimand issued to him at the Komsomol meeting in his labour collective.

"In the first place, I'm responsible for my passengers and I keep my eyes on the road. I have one boss already, so what do I need these party hacks for? And in the second place, if not for that reprimand, I'd have had a new trolleybus in a month's time."

Lizka watched Artur as he spoke and she was absolutely enchanted by the way he ate. When he burnt his mouth on the hot pea soup, he snuffled loudly, drawing the mucus back up his nose, and he broke the bread up into little pieces with his strong hands blackened by engine oil, and then greedily despatched them into his smiling mouth. He was so bold and good-natured and straightforward: Lizka really liked him a lot, and she accepted his invitation to go to the cinema with him.

Outside the cinema they met his friends from the trolleybus depot, a boisterous group of men and women drinking beer and cracking jokes.

"Hi! Are you Artur's girlfriend?" a girl shouted in Lizka's ear and thrust a bottle of beer into her hand. "I'm Vera. Have you got an inside pocket?"

"What?" Vera asked, puzzled.

"I'm telling you, stick the bottle in your inside pocket. They don't let you in with beer."

Lizka glanced round at Artur, who was standing in the queue for tickets, shrugged and hid the bottle inside her jacket. The group didn't pay any particular attention to Lizka, because they were all talking to each other at once and laughing. There was nothing else Lizka could do but listen to the jokes with a smile on her face. She liked these people too and she wanted to join in the conversation somehow, but she suddenly realised that after all that time with Victor she'd forgotten how to talk to normal people. Not knowing what to say, she asked Vera: "Is this the way you always enjoy yourselves?"

"No, just sometimes on Fridays. On pay day."

Just then the bell rang and they all set off towards the entrance.

"Granny Zoya's on ticket duty again today!" Artur shouted as he ran to catch up, and the entire group exploded in a new roar of laughter.

When she saw the trolleybus group, the little old pensioner checking tickets at the entrance threw her arms out wide and started wailing tearfully: "You again! I won't let you in! Not with beer, I won't. Last time you wouldn't let people watch the film, and I can see you're already half-cut today. I won't let you in with beer!"

But the group refused to surrender, and they crowded round the old woman.

"You can frisk us, Granny Zoya, we haven't got any beer with us. Word of honour! It's all inside already."

"How's your health, Granny Zoya?"

"How's your rheumatism?"

Gently moving the old woman aside, they all rushed into the hall and dashed to grab places in the back row. Lizka and Artur sat together in the row in front and regretted it from the very start of the film. They had to listen to the whispering, jeers and indecent comments from behind.

"Where's the film from?"

"It's Italian."

"I think I've already seen it on video. There'll be big tits."

"No, there won't."

"Yes, there will, you'll see!"

"Our censor cut them out."

"Want to bet?"

"What?"

"A crate of beer."

And then they started playing at "meteorites". The trolleybus crews tore their tickets into little scraps, crumpled them up and threw them into the beam of the projector. At every new burst Granny Zoya jumped up off her chair beside the door she was guarding, but she couldn't bring herself to walk into the darkness, and she just waved her fist threateningly and sank back down again to the sound of friendly laughter and clinking bottles from the back row.

And in the forty-second minute of the film, with a shower of "meteorites" overhead, Artur put his hand on Lizka's and asked her to marry him. He told her he worked on route eleven, the one Lizka took every morning to get from her home to her job. He had fallen in love with her two weeks earlier and several times he'd swapped shifts with his partner so that he could admire her in the mirror above his windscreen. He confessed that it hadn't been hard to figure out where she worked, that leaving the Komsomol had been a planned move, intended to impress her with his boldness and win her heart, and that he was very shy, which was why he'd chosen a dark cinema to make his declaration of love. Lizka was glad that he couldn't see her embarrassment and the way she lowered her eyes and blushed at these words that touched her heart, words she was hearing for the first time in her life. She was filled with a pleasant, warm glow at knowing that she was loved and overwhelmed by an inexplicable feeling of gratitude to Artur. But he added that he didn't want to hurry her and he would wait for her answer as long as it took.

After the film the trolleybus group invited them to the nearest beer bar, but Lizka was feeling anxious about Victor and she hurried home. Artur didn't want to part with Lizka so he set off across the park with her to see her on her way.

As they walked slowly along the pathway that was already free of ice they could see islets of blackened snow on both sides; the voices of the birds and the sound of falling water-drops were carried a long way on the warm spring breeze, filling their hearts with joy and putting them in a playful mood. Lizka suddenly ran off, hid behind a tree and made a snowball, then threw it at Artur. He laughed and threw a handful of snow back at her. Lizka wanted him to kiss her, and she thought up a provocative plan. She would start to run and pretend to slip, he would catch her in his arms, their faces would move close and he would kiss her. It was a good plan, and Lizka went dashing off. She heard someone catching up with her, breathing heavily through his nose, and she was just going to pretend to fall, when suddenly a black, shaggy monster knocked her to the ground and she saw a massive young German shepherd dog standing over her, pressing her into a cold puddle with its dirty paws, and Artur and the dog's owner were hurrying towards them.

"Max, bad boy! No!"

While the dog's owner made profuse apologies and Artur and Lizka wiped the mud off her jacket with their handkerchiefs, the culprit circled round them, jumping up with a loud bark or lying down on his front paws and wagging his tail or trying to lick their faces.

"He's still very young and not trained yet, and he's just interested in everything. I'm very sorry."

But Lizka wasn't upset at all, she just laughed. Her plan worked anyway, because when the man with the dog had gone, Artur took her frozen little hands in his big driver's hands and kissed her tenderly on the lips.

As they said goodnight, they agreed that every morning Lizka would wait for his trolleybus at the stop outside her house at exactly seven thirty-five.

When Lizka got home, Victor could not help noticing the change in her behaviour. She was happy and mysterious, smiling at her own thoughts, and so preoccupied that she couldn't do anything right.

"Why did you leave without finishing your work?" Victor was

furious, but he was restraining himself. "All our country's problems are caused by irresponsible people like you."

"More likely by hypocrites like you and your gang," Lizka retorted. "Did Alla tell you?"

"Yes, she did. Unlike you, she's well disciplined and loyal too. Where have you been?"

"I went to the cinema with some girlfriends. Isn't that allowed?"

"Not during working hours!" Victor said, outraged. "You have to understand that what you need to think about right now is getting into a college, not wasting your youth on idle amusement with your worthless girlfriends."

"All right, calm down, will you!" Lizka said, thinking to herself that next time she'd lie and say she'd been studying in the library.

It's impossible to say how things would have gone for Artur and Lizka if Victor had kept a check on her free time. But the following week he was due to go to another town on business, and Lizka was very glad indeed about that.

Now she hopped in through the front doors of Artur's trolleybus every morning, and they agreed where to meet and how to spend the evening. Artur painted their future life together in bright rainbow colours, and as Lizka got to know him better and better she gradually began to feel inclined to accept his proposal. They could live in the room he had in a communal apartment, it was big enough for two. In the summer they could live in his parents' apartment – they were away at the dacha for the entire season when they could work in their vegetable garden. The only thing that didn't suit Artur was Lizka's present job.

"You'll see your ex every day, and I'll feel jealous. You could get a job with the trolleybus office, they need traffic controllers," he said, trying to persuade her.

"And maybe I could drive a trolleybus?" Lizka asked. "My mum said my granddad was a driver."

"That's a great idea!" Artur said happily. "Although driving skills aren't inherited. Then we'd be together all the time – at home and at work. My friends are a lively bunch. We'll go to the cinema, the discotheques, the beer bars, have picnics out in the country. It will all be absolutely wonderful! And the most important thing is, I love you. Will you marry me?"

"Yes."

When Victor came back from his business trip, Lizka was waiting for him with her suitcases packed. The two suitcases from Lopukhov had been joined by two new ones and a large travelling bag. Artur had borrowed a friend's car and was waiting for her downstairs.

"Hi."

"Hi."

Realising what was happening, Victor became rather sullen and upset, but he still held out the flowers and the box he had brought with him.

"This is for you. Trainers."

"Don't bother. I'm leaving."

"Take them anyway. They're your size."

"Keep them for your next girlfriend."

"There won't be a new one any time soon, so you take them."

"Thank you." Lizka put the box into her bag and tried to smile, but her smile turned out sour and unnatural.

She wanted to tell him that she felt gratitude and affection for him, but she didn't love him at all and so she didn't want to make him suffer. But on the other hand, she wanted to tell him that his entire life and his work were riddled with lies and contempt for other people, that she was a simple person and she wanted to be with simple people; she felt more comfortable with them. She had been intending to deliver an entire hard-hitting speech with that air of confidence he had tried to teach her, but now, as she looked at him, she couldn't do it.

"Will you have some tea with me?" Victor asked.

"Someone's waiting for me. Sorry."

"Who is he?" Victor enquired.

"A nice young guy."

"Youth is naïve and full of rash decisions."

"He's proposed to me."

"Well, well." Victor was unable to conceal his surprise. "Isn't it a bit quick?"

"I love him," Lizka, and suddenly felt a dangerous thought flash through her head: did she really love Artur?

"Love and being in love are different things, and your infantile…" Victor began, but Lizka interrupted him.

"There's no point in trying. I'm not going to stay…"

"All right, it's your life. Be happy." He kissed her goodbye on the forehead and helped carry her things to the lift.

Nina took responsibility for organising the wedding. She grabbed the opportunity enthusiastically with both hands, because she still hadn't married her architect, whose granny stubbornly refused to die and leave them the apartment. The entire cost was borne by Artur's parents and at the very last moment Lizka, who hadn't wanted to tell her mother anything about the wedding at first, sent an invitation to Lopukhov after all. She decided not to invite her esoteric aunt in the kimono. And she simply didn't have any other relatives.

On one side there were girlish tears of joy, the magic of a brilliant white dress, the anxious waiting, the intimate, heartfelt chatter and kisses from girlfriends, and on the other the final drunken evenings with friends, slaps on the shoulder, rueful regret that the ranks of madcap bachelors had been diminished and thoughtful finger exercises on the pocket calculator – and then, after two weeks of frantic activity, at the appointed day and hour, everything was calm and quiet.

The bride's army, led by their chief of staff, Nina, occupied an advantageous position in the hostel. Lizka herself, standing on a stool in her wedding dress with one shoe on, had been locked in the room farthest from the entrance, which the supervisor of the hostel had kindly lent for this festive occasion. The first line of defence, which ran across the entrance to the hostel, consisted of ladies who were perhaps not very young, but had a thorough knowledge of the subtle traditional details of the ransoming of a bride. The second defensive position was on the staircase, where the cunning students of the medical college were gathered. The last and most significant line of fortifications was controlled by Nina herself. These fortifications were located directly in front of the bride's room and consisted of an impenetrable wall formed by forty of the most enchanting inhabitants of the hostel. The entrance to the room itself was mined with three three-litre jars containing dark beer, kvass and home brew. The attackers had to drain their contents in order to obtain the key to the room. They wouldn't be told which of the three jars the key was in. The plumber Tolya, one of Nina's three lovers, had even suggested felling a couple of trees on the street, so that the enemy couldn't approach the building in a vehicle, but the supervisor had thought this excessive.

The bridegroom's retinue arrived at the field of battle in five cars and a minibus. Artur had appointed his friend Sergei as his senior deputy, since he had already been a witness at many weddings and demonstrated great ingenuity. The actual assault group consisted of friends and colleagues, that is, almost all the men from trolleybus depot number four.

In strict observance of national tradition, with songs accompanied by an accordion and humorous badinage, they had no great difficulty in breaking through the first-stage defences. But the resistance in the stairwell was stubborn. On every single one of the forty-eight steps the bridegroom had to think up a term of affection for his bride, and then identify the lips of his beloved among a dozen different lipstick imprints. There were so many tasks of this kind that Artur was afraid they would be late for the registry office, until he called on his friends to assist him and they managed, working with gentle but serious persistence, to push their way through and reach the top of the stairs and the final bulwark – Nina and her friends. The assault immediately became bogged down. The witness Sergei knew from previous experience that the bridegroom would be obliged to lay down several metres of money, and he had made Artur change a certain sum into the smallest possible denominations, so that he had a whole sack of notes. But he hadn't been prepared for the cunning of the ever-resourceful Nina. Every time the bridegroom, crawling on all fours, came close to the solid wall formed by the girls, they took a step backwards. There wasn't enough money, arguments were ineffective and, at the risk of really being late for the Palace of Weddings, they had to run to the nearest shop to change more. Nina observed Sergei's confusion in triumph, but her joy was premature. When the line of money reached the jars with the key from the bride's room, Sergei set one of them to his mouth, shook it gently and, pretending that that it had slipped, deftly dropped it on the two others. In the twinkling of an eye he bent down and picked up the key from among the shards of glass with his little finger. The two chiefs of staff exchanged glances again and it was clear to everyone how this pair would spend the night.

The search for the shoe hidden in the ceiling lamp took a long time, but they found it and they weren't late for the registry office.

The portly lady in the dark blue dress reaching down to the floor, with a heavy crest of the USSR hanging at her breast, rolled her eyes and spoke with an affected passion that made her seem like some terrible enchantress reading a spell. Lizka didn't take in any of the words; she was so nervous that she was trembling all over, and her hand shook as she signed her name. For some reason she looked at her mother, who had arrived a day before the wedding and was standing there arm-in-arm with a strange man and smiling with moist eyes. From the man's suit, Lizka realised that he had also come from Lopukhov. She didn't want to pretend that he was her father, but she kept quiet when he kissed her, in order not to disrupt the solemn event. Her dear mother, older now, with her vulgar lipstick and, as ever, with a man. Why had they never talked about anything serious?

Artur's parents, embarrassed but proud, accepted all the congratulations and were swamped with flowers. Lizka remembered the first time she had met them.

"Dad, Mum, this is my fiancée, Liza."

"Hello."

Artur's father, an ex-colonel, had scrutinised Lizka in a way that made her palms start sweating, but then he had smiled exactly like Artur.

"I don't bite. Our son's choice is our choice too. Come in. Make yourself at home."

"You've heard about the Tatars, I suppose? Muslim laws and all the rest," said Artur's mother, sticking her head out of the kitchen.

"Don't worry, we became russified long ago, except that they still don't let women into the Tatar cemetery. Will you help me with the salads?"

Kind, friendly people like that couldn't have raised a bad son. They were so happy today, she didn't want to let them down.

The ceremony came to an end. Lizka gasped as her legs were swept up into the air and she was left with no choice but to grab hold of Artur's strong neck. It was the first time she'd been carried in someone's arms, the first time she'd had a ring on her finger, and she was surrounded by all these people who meant so much to her and did so much for her! Victor Mikhailovich could never have done anything like this. That arrogant egotist who could only talk about himself and his own pains. How she wished he could see her now.

The banquet was held in the trolleybus depot canteen and was a wonderful success, with enough vodka for everyone. Someone fell asleep with his face in his plate, someone went home with someone else's wife, the witness Sergei got his sleeve torn off in a drunken brawl, but the newlyweds didn't see any of that. They left early and spent their entire wedding night unpacking presents, opening envelopes and counting money.

Lizka liked her new family life. She eagerly set about making Artur's room comfortable with meticulous attention to detail and an imagination that seemed to have appeared from nowhere. She cleaned and tidied, often moved the furniture about, changed the curtains. She wanted to make use of many of the things she had seen in Victor Mikhailovich's apartment. She asked one of their neighbours, a carpenter, to make her a shelf out of an old ironing board, and when it was ready she was absolutely delighted with her new item of furniture.

"These old carpets trap such a lot of dust. Let's throw them out altogether and put in a new floor. I want lacquered parquet," she suggested to Artur.

"Excellent! I'll have a word with a decorator I know. And in general, you just make things the way you like them, wife."

Wife. The word gave her such a warm, happy feeling. She wasn't just a young woman now – she was a wife. She had her own home now and the entry she'd been longing for in her passport.

"I just wanted to know if you objected, husband!"

He smiled when she said that, put his arms round her and kissed her: "Yes, I'm your husband."

After that they often addressed each other in that way, half-joking and laughing, but proud of the fact.

"I glad you like to take trouble over the room; I haven't got any taste at all. But you should save your imagination for the apartment we're going to have. Since we're both going to work we're bound to get one. Especially since Gorbachev has promised every Soviet citizen a separate apartment in the year 2000."

Her very own apartment! That was what she wanted. Only there were still eleven years to go to the year 2000! But then, on the other hand, what did eleven years mean to hearts that were in love?

After she left her job with the municipal party committee, Lizka studied the newspapers again, wondering what college she could enrol in, and looking for work. She managed the household perfectly and always had a tasty supper ready for Artur when he came home, but she could feel money was tight and she didn't want to be a burden to him. And apart from that, now that she was independent, she felt totally transformed and needed somewhere to apply her energy. She wanted to do something, create something, make herself and her husband happy.

"Tell me, Artur, what do people live for?"

"How should I know? Everybody just lives, and so do we. It's nature."

"But I always feel there should be something more. Is that normal?"

"Everybody wants something more. But why have you suddenly got this bee in your bonnet?"

"I don't know. I suppose at first I didn't have anything at all, and now it seems like I have everything, but I still want something more. I want people to be kinder and more romantic…"

"Everybody wants that. Let's go to sleep."

Artur would turn his back to Lizka and fall asleep quickly, and she couldn't help recalling Victor Mikhailovich. Of course, he had been more interesting. He could talk about subjects like that for hours, especially when he was sitting in his beloved armchair with a bottle of good wine. Supper by candlelight and wonderful walks – there had been something poetic about him. One day, when they were out walking they'd seen a man who was walking by slip and fall and Lizka hadn't been able to stop herself laughing, but Victor had exclaimed: "How painful it must be for someone to fall and strike his bones against the icy asphalt! It's not just a physical pain, it's the pain caused by other people's malicious delight. Someone only has to stumble and we're overcome by an honest, heart-warming joy at our neighbour's misfortune. How we revel in violence and how incapable we are of taking pride in people who can make a better job of something than we do."

Lizka had understood him in her own way. And she had liked the feeling that the second secretary of the municipal party committee was talking to her, trusting her with his thoughts and feelings. He was powerful, but she had the power over him in bed. And this one just said: "Let's go to sleep."

Could it really have been a rash move and a terrible mistake to surrender Victor to some other woman's arms and exchange him for this handsome boy who loved her? But then, Victor would never have proposed to her, and so she hadn't given him up for a boy, she'd swapped him for a husband.

Let's go to sleep. Well, she really did need to sleep.

When Artur came back from work the next day he had a serious air.

"I've been thinking over what you said about wanting something more. How about children?"

The question caught Lizka off-guard. She knew there was something not right with her body, but she didn't know why.

"I need to think about it," she answered quickly, feeling her ears turning red, and she decided she would definitely see a doctor straight away.

"What's there to think about? Children are the flowers of our life. Let's have a whole flower-bed! The men at the depot might grumble that their kids don't let them get enough sleep, but they're really glad to be dads."

"You know, I don't want to hurry, and then it would be a bit crowded in this room for three." Lizka was very upset and she could hardly conceal it, because she didn't really know how to lie. "I'll give you an answer later, darling, not now."

Tormented by the terrible idea that Artur would leave her if she couldn't have children, she strained to follow the doctor's handwriting, which only he could understand. The gynaecologist looked up and asked gently: "Do you have any friends or relatives abroad?"

"I beg your pardon?"

"Don't worry, for goodness' sake. You can easily get pregnant after a two-week course of medication. The only problem is that our pharmacies don't have any hormonal preparations. If you can get hold of them, come back again with your husband. Here's the list."

Lizka was convinced that the doctor was right after she had been round a dozen pharmacies in the city and received no reply except a smile of sympathy or the spiteful enquiry: "Where are you from, Mars?" She thought about asking Victor, who could get hold of anything at all, and he would definitely have done it for her, but she decided not to out of pride. She didn't tell Artur about her terrible problem, or even Nina; she suffered the torment all alone. She felt as if the idea of a child was becoming an obsession and tearing her apart inside, and she couldn't just be a housewife any longer. And although Artur had offered to help her get a job as a traffic controller, and she went to the trolleybus office intending to do that, what she actually did was something quite different.

SIX

THE COUNTRY HAD gone insane yet again. Following an old habit with roots going back centuries, they were demolishing the old without the slightest idea of what the new would be like. People climbed on to tanks and fell under them, littered the streets with barricades and leaflets, pounded their chests with their fists, yelled and sobbed and laughed, pelted each other with microphones, bottles and their own convictions. Moscow was seething and the provinces were buying up salt and matches wholesale. They changed the state crest and national flag and swapped one old political party for a hundred new ones. As usual, they suddenly remembered that they'd forgotten all about food and yet again they delved into the people's pockets, and the people sighed and swore submissively and once again, with a naïve faith in the new tsar, gave everything they had. Then they began sharing things out – in the wild, expansive Russian manner, with drunken passion and the spilling of blood. No one knew when they would stop, calm down and take a look around.

The country had gone insane, but the bright green trolleybus number seventeen was still trundling round the wide streets of the city of G. It had stopped raining now, and shimmering glints of pale October sunshine were reflected on the trolleybus's windows from the newly formed puddles and the sparse, wet autumn foliage. It was nine o'clock in the morning, the rush hour was coming to an end, and the trolleybus was half-empty. The sound of the motor working was so smooth and monotonous that Lizka, who had slept badly, almost closed her eyes. There were hardly any stops on Industrial Street, and apart from the short stretch in front of the mechanical engineering plant, there were no potholes in the asphalt surface here. You could feel that straight away, because the old vehicle that just been through a major service stopped shaking and rattling. Lizka had almost fallen into a doze, but her hands still automatically swung the huge wheel to the left just before Factory Lane. She suddenly realised where she was, pinched her thigh with her nails and braked sharply. The nose of the trolleybus was sticking out a long way over the line and, as she looked down, Liza saw the driver behind the windscreen of a Lada that was driving round her waving his hands at her angrily and moving his mouth in soundless abuse.

"Yes, I know, I know! Go on, will you, you freak!" Lizka let the truck that was following the Lada go by and then turned. Then she looked in her mirror to see whether her little mistake had had any consequences in the passenger compartment and, once she was sure the passengers were still chatting away as light-heartedly as ever or gazing idly out of the windows, she calmed down again.

The reason for her sleepless night, of course, was Artur. Just recently he'd lost interest in her as a woman and he'd been making love to her less often and with less variety. When she'd tried taking a friend's advice and flirting with other men in front of him in order to reawaken his interest in her, he'd made a jealous scene and back at home they'd quarrelled all night long. Where had that boy who loved her so much gone? And, apart from that, it probably wasn't right anyway for a husband and wife to work together in trolleybus depot number 4, both of them as drivers – but there had been a time when he was keen on the idea and he'd even helped her to learn.

"Are you all right?" the conductress Liubasha asked, sticking her head in through the half-open door that separated the driver's cabin from the passenger compartment.

"Yes, I was just thinking."

"About Artur?"

Lizka nodded.

"Don't let it get you down. Look what I've got!" Liubasha pulled a roll of tickets out of her pocket. "When shall we start?"

"After this round," Lizka said in a happier voice. "There won't be any inspectors then."

Selling tickets "on the side" had been a common practice for many drivers of public transport vehicles for a long time, and the bus drivers also used to sell off surplus petrol. Their wages were always falling behind the price of food, and sometimes they weren't even paid for months at a time. So even the bosses turned a blind eye to the fact that only seventy per cent of total receipts actually found its way into the till. The girls had adopted their male colleagues' methods, but they only resorted to such measures when it was absolutely necessary.

This time they needed the money for a party that Liubasha was having at her place on Wednesday, when a third of the women drivers and conductresses at depot number 4 had a day off. When they decided not to have any men at the party, Lizka had been glad to agree. She already knew about Artur's adventures, when he used the excuse of repairing his trolleybus to spend the evening with male and female friends in bars and saunas, and this was her little revenge. The other girls who were supposed to come to the hen party – apart from herself and Liubasha, who had just recently divorced her husband because of his drinking – were their colleagues Vera and Irina, Lizka's partner Katya and the doctor Zoya Andreevna, who checked the drivers' state of health every morning.

The trolleybus slowly crawled up on to the top of Lazy Hill and the gleaming wet roofs and streets of the city of G came into sight below. Braking gently just before yet another hole in the road, Lizka thought that she really loved this city, except, of course, for the road-workers. A Lada number 5 came dashing towards her with Vera at the wheel, waving to her. Lizka smiled in reply and blinked her indicator. Up ahead, where the central district of the city began, she could see the walls of the old monastery.

Just before Mikhailovsky Market, Lizka managed to dash through a yellow light, overtake two buses and halt at the stop before them. Liubasha went dashing to her conductor's seat, afraid of being crushed by the flood of new passengers forcing their way into the trolleybus. There were always a lot of people here and even after desperate efforts to cram everyone in, the trolleybus still couldn't hold them all by a long way. The doors closed with difficulty and in her mirror Lizka saw one of the passengers left standing on the pavement lash out at them angrily with his foot.

"Citizens! Please pay for your journey promptly," Liubasha appealed to them, hoping that everyone would ask his neighbour to hand on his money, but every time she said this the citizens would put on innocent faces and pretend they hadn't the slightest idea that there was even a conductor on the bus. Liubasha sighed and began using her elbows to force a way through to the back platform.

Just before the next stop Lizka braked sharply several times and then moved on just as suddenly, packing her passengers together more tightly. At least another ten would fit in now.

In the conditions of the new market economy an undeclared war was being waged between the trolleybus depots and the bus routes for every single client. With their low engine speed, the trolleybuses overtook the buses going uphill and on the level stretches of road, while the buses exploited the trolleybuses' dependence on their overhead cables. Drivers spoke to each other on their cabin radios, cut in front of each other and deliberately held each other up. Lizka knew many of her competitors by sight, and she always fought against them with a smile on her face. If, for instance, she was driving uphill and she overtook a bus, she deliberately wouldn't let it go past her. The bus lost speed, had to switch down to a lower gear and was soon left far behind. But the bus drivers knew the locations of all the electrical connections, where a trolleybus had to brake in order to switch over on to its own branch of the power network. And then they overtook Lizka, smiling at her through their windscreens with malicious delight. Sometimes she got so carried away in the heat of the struggle that her boom came off the cable. And then, to the hooting of car horns and the muttering of passengers who were always late to get somewhere, she had to get out of the trolleybus and use the rope to put the boom back in place.

A red light lit up on her dashboard. Lizka drew in to the kerb and opened the doors. To help them in their fight against passengers travelling without tickets, the girls had asked the depot's electrician to install a button under the conductor's seat that Liubasha could press when she wanted to put passengers off who didn't pay. If one of these "hares" refused to leave the trolleybus voluntarily, then Lizka simply waited for the other passengers to persuade him to go. Halts like this disrupted the timetable, and once Liubasha and Lizka had even forfeited their bonus as a result, but they stuck with this method as a matter of principle.

They didn't have to wait long. A drunken tramp carrying a

plastic bag full of empty bottles and wearing one shoe was pushed out of the rear door. Another one went flying out after him.

"Next stop – Karl Marx Street," Lizka announced into the microphone and smiled involuntarily. She had always found this part of the route amusing, and in her own mind she thought of it as "the German stretch".

The stops that came after Karl Marx Street were: Friedrich Engels Street, Klara Zetkin Street, Rosa Luxemburg Street, Erich Weinert Lane and Ernst Telman Square. In the early nineties they'd tried to rename them, but the new names hadn't taken, and they caused constant confusion. Some of the houses had the old street-signs and some had the new ones. The passengers often asked Liubasha to explain things to them, but she just shrugged and suggested they should ask the older people in the trolleybus.

Lizka spotted a red trolleybus, a number 11, in the distance, at the stop on the other side of the street. Artur could quite easily be driving it; he drove a red one too. Lizka decided to look away when were passing each other. Damn it, she had to do something about their relationship. Maybe she should be unfaithful once or twice, to bring him down a peg or two.

The number 11 went rushing past furiously, splashing mud up on to Lizka's windscreen. It was Artur.

At last, there was Gagarin Street. Lizka drove into the turning circle and looked at her watch. There was just over fifteen minutes left until her next run. She gave her sandwiches to Liubasha, knowing from experience that a full stomach would only make her feel so sleepy she couldn't resist, and decided to make do with coffee from her thermos flask and a cigarette.

"Listen, Liubash, maybe I ought to be unfaithful to my husband, eh?"

"It won't do any good," said Liubashka, fishing the remains of her salad out of the plastic jar and licking her fork. "You won't be able to hide it anyway, he'll find out and apply for a divorce. Then you'll be out on the street again."

"What am I going to do?"

"Re-educate him. The old men are like melons – they grow a fat belly, their little stalk dries up and they can't be trained, but yours is still young."

"So how do I re-educate him?"

"Well, maybe you should be more mysterious, encourage a healthy feeling of jealousy…"

"Thanks. Yesterday's scene was enough. He broke my favourite cup."

"That's right. What man's going to like it if his woman gets flirty with other men? They're terribly possessive of their own property. You're already too eman…emancir…anyway, you show how independent you are too often. They don't like that. For instance, why do you think foreigners have started marrying our girls recently? Because in the West all their women are emancirp…anyway, they're getting more and more like men." Liubasha stuffed a sandwich into her mouth.

"It's easy for you to talk. You divorced your man, and now you're telling other people what to do."

"I didn't want anything from that cretin apart from a child and half his property," said Liubasha, remembering her ex-husband. Then she started angrily telling Lizka about his faults and how he'd ruined her life. And, as usual, the girls agreed that all men are motherfuckers and liars, and then they agreed that Liubasha should get hold of as many illegal tickets as possible, so they could get enough money for a radio cassette. Then they could install it in their trolleybus and fight their sleepiness and bad mood with loud, energetic music.

It began drizzling, and the wheel of trolleybus number 17 made a soft, champing sound as it drove back out into the street. Lizka wasn't so fond of the other half of the circle, or rather, the other circle of the large figure eight that made up her route. It ran through the old city, where the traffic was even livelier and the streets were narrower. Trolleybuses and buses couldn't overtake each other here, and they were hindered by the trams and the frantically bustling pedestrians who caused traffic jams and "road transport incidents". Lizka had a presentiment that something bad was about to happen, and she tried hard to shake off her distracted mood as she concentrated hard on the traffic, let one more crazy driver go past and slowly set off along her lane.

Her presentiment had not deceived her. At the stop in front of the puppet theatre she heard a thump. Lizka turned cold and her eyes dashed from one mirror to the other. Standing up behind the steering wheel, she saw a man lying beside her front wheel and exclaimed furiously: "How can you stop in time when these cattle dash for the doors like that? The idiots!"

She jumped out into the street, followed by Liubasha. The man was lying on the kerb without moving, with his cap beside him, and there was a thin trickle of blood coming from his nose.

"My God, he's dead," Liubasha wailed.

"Shut up!" Lizka said, paying no attention to the onlookers gaping at her. She squatted down beside the man and checked his pulse. "The special accident unit's only six stops from here. Help me!"

The girls dragged the injured man, who was still unconscious, in through the front door. Lizka was shaking, but she tried to get a grip on herself.

"Please accept our apologies. For technical reasons, this trolleybus will not be going any further. Please vacate the passenger compartment," she announced through the microphone in a strange voice that wasn't hers, and as soon as the last passenger had got out, she put her foot down. "Liubasha, look for the sal ammoniac in the first-aid kit!"

The situation was perfectly clear to Lizka. The man had come too close to the edge of the pavement and he'd been knocked down by the side mirror. She had been driving up to the stop quite slowly, and the blow couldn't have been a hard one. But then, who could tell?

While Lizka was manoeuvring between astonished drivers in their private cars and overtaking at high speed, Liubasha held a piece of cotton wool soaked in sal ammoniac up to the man's nose. The man grimaced and opened his eyes.

"Thank God we didn't kill you," Liubasha told him in a delighted voice.

The man tried to get up, but immediately slumped back on to the seat.

"Thank you. I actually saw the mirror coming for me," he said, wiping away the blood under his nose with a handkerchief. "I just didn't have time to get out of the way. Because of my leg. It doesn't work too well."

"Did you hurt your leg?"

"Yes, I mean, no. I hurt it a long time ago, I got a piece of shrapnel through it."

Lizka stopped at the hospital.

"How did you know I was just on my way to this hospital?" the man asked in surprise.

"We didn't know. I just thought that after an accident like that you ought to see a doctor," Lizka replied, secretly glad that he was already feeling better. "We'll go in with you in, I'll just take my boom down so the others can get past."

"No thank you, I'll manage on my own. I have to show my leg to the surgeon in any case and, believe me, a plain ordinary concussion is nothing new to me."

"Here's your cap."

"Thank you. But where's my stick?"

"Your stick?"

"Yes, I walk with a stick because my leg hurts."

"We must have left it behind because we were in such a rush," said Lizka, glancing at Liubasha, but Liubasha just shrugged. "Well, then, we'll buy you a new one. What's your name?"

"Maxim. You can just call me Max."

"All right, Max, tell me your phone number, and we'll do it today…"

"No, no, absolutely not. What happened was my fault and anyway, you don't know what height I am."

"Then tell me, Max, do you have any claims to make against us?" Lizka asked uncertainly. "I mean, you won't be making any complaints to the traffic police or the management of the trolleybus depot?"

"Hmm…" said Max, looking at the driver's badge with her name on it. "Only on one condition, Liza."

"What's that?"

"That you have dinner with me some evening. How about tomorrow at nine in the 'Lily of the Valley'?"

Either because she was in such a hurry – the cars behind them were sounding their horns furiously – or because she felt that she owed this man something, Lizka agreed. And Liubasha gave a broad smile, exposing her large front teeth.

Lizka finished her route without any passengers, switched off the engine and decided to call her partner Katya and get her to stand in for her. Now that the accident was behind her, Lizka could feel her hands beginning to shake. She'd been through similar situations a dozen times, and she knew she shouldn't drive in this state. She kept seeing what had happened over and over again in every last detail, and she was tormented by the idea of what would have happened if Maxim had been killed.

In order to avoid any problems, she and Liubasha decided not to say anything to anyone, and so when Katya arrived, Lizka said she had some urgent business to see to and handed over the trolleybus in a very matter-of-fact way: "The left side of the middle doors sometimes gets stuck and the right front wheel is pulling slightly to one side. It would be a good idea to have it balanced again."

Katya could sense that Lizka was nervous, but she didn't ask any questions. She had a small child who was often unwell, and Lizka had stood in for her more than once.

Lizka didn't want to go home, because Artur would come back soon. Even if she tried talking to him about what had happened today and looking for support and reassurance, she wasn't likely to get it.

"You have to watch the road and not sit there nattering with the conductor!" That was what he'd say, of course, and then he'd be sure to add: "Oh God! I'm so sick of these women drivers!"

And then he'd start yelling, waving his arms about and hurling reproaches at her.

But Lizka did go home after all, and in order to cheer herself up a bit, she ate two big bars of chocolate, which made her feel sick. Tea, a sleeping pill and bed. How glad she was that this crazy, dangerous, almost unreal day had come to an end.

Lizka curled up tight and tried to fall asleep, but for some reason she remembered her third wedding anniversary. She had collected a whole sackful of fallen leaves out in the country – reddish-grey ones, bright-red ones and brown ones, from an oak tree, an ash tree and a maple – they were incredibly beautiful. Then she'd tipped them out on to their conjugal bed, mixed up with bunches of mountain ash and white apple blossom. She'd been lying on the bed, waiting for Artur to come home, she had wine and candles, but all he'd done was frown and ask what kind of stupid nonsense this was, dragging all sorts of rubbish into the house.

Lizka's thoughts wouldn't let her relax, and her body felt tense.

Marriage contracts had only just begun to appear then, but if they'd existed earlier, Lizka would definitely have included one important point in hers. Her husband would have had to give her a back massage every day – from the cervical vertebrae down to the coccyx, and kiss her feet. And that was all she would have wanted from her husband. As well as not using coarse language. And football only once a month, and beer only once a month too! And then...

"That's great!" Artur exclaimed when he saw Lizka in the bed, and deliberately slammed the door loudly. "You might at least have cooked something before you went to bed. This is the second day without a hot meal!"

He began rummaging in the fridge, and Lizka felt like telling him to get stuffed. But if she said that, he'd stop her getting a proper night's rest again. So she kept quiet, pretending to be sleeping, until she really did fall asleep.

The next evening Lizka arrived at the "Lily of the Valley" full of the joyful anticipation of something new. The idea of being unfaithful to her husband had taken an even stronger hold on her mind, and she wasn't going to resist if Maxim showed any

initiative. Still not knowing who was sitting beside her at the table
– a road accident victim or a future lover – she flirted with him
without any great originality and tried to ask more questions than
she answered.

"Your leg. Where did you injure it?"

"In the war," Max replied, as if it that was something absolutely
obvious.

"You were down there, in the south?"

"Yes, and I want to go back again; my friends are still there, but
the doctors won't let me."

"Tell me, were you really afraid there?"

"Well, maybe just at the beginning. But later I had a good time.
We drank vodka and smoked dope, sometimes we fired our guns."

"Who at?"

"Everybody." Max had suddenly turned serious. "Let's not talk
about that."

The waitress brought them young roast chickens and cognac.

"Look, it's brand new," said Max, taking his stick out from
under the table and showing it to Lizka. "We should drink to the
new acquisition."

"I didn't want to knock you down at all," said Lizka, feeling
sincerely sorry for what had happened.

"I know that. Here's to a happy ending!"

They drank. Music with a strong beat started to play and the
small dance floor filled up with dancing teenagers.

"Would you like me to tell you about my first accident?" Lizka
asked in a jollier voice.

"Yes."

"I was driving the training bus with my instructor. Some New
Russian cut straight across me and I caught him with my bumper.

He got out and started swearing, so I got out as well, with the instructor…"

The dream was always the same. An armoured personnel carrier driving down a gravel road. He's sitting up on the armour plating with everyone else, naked to the waist, basking in the dry, warm wind. All of them are dreaming of getting to the stream as soon as possible so that they can get a wash and slake their thirst. On every side there are fragrant trees surrounded by luscious grass. Then the vehicle comes to a sudden halt: there's a shell crate lying all on its own in the road ahead. The sappers are the first to jump down on to the ground. They approach the crate slowly and cautiously squat down beside it. Max can't see what they're doing, but he is overcome by a sudden feeling of alarm. His sweaty hand clutches the butt of his rifle tighter and tighter, and he strains his eyes to see into the hills around them. Suddenly one of the sappers dashes to the side of the road, goes down on all fours and starts puking. Everybody goes running to the crate. Including Max.

There are two severed legs lying there, one on each side of the head, and two crossed arms below it. Max recognises the head; it's Kolya from the second platoon, they used to play chess together. He went missing three days earlier. Head, legs, arms. But where's his body? Where's his body?

And then Max would wake up. And he couldn't get to sleep again, he just sat there smoking and gazing at the ceiling until morning.

"…and while we were waiting for the cops, he kept threatening me with working for the rest of my life to pay for getting his car fixed." Liza was still telling her story and, to judge by her laughter, it was a very amusing one.

"Let's drink," Max suggested.

"Okay."

They had another drink and Lizka continued, but Max gazed past her to one side, at the bar counter. The customers were chatting light-heartedly with each other, twitching in time to the music. Some fat character ran his piggy eyes over the dance floor and whispered something into the ears of the two ladies standing beside him. The ladies laughed hysterically. Maxim clenched his fist under the table. Who were they laughing at? At him?

The mercenaries never got any blood on their hands. They used to put a wire frame over the prisoner's head first, before they cut it off. While he was still alive. Then they hung the frame with the head on a rocket launcher and fired it at the Russians. The heads would go tumbling along over the ground. Very often men's genitals came flying in too.

One day they caught an Arab mercenary and started giving him "a ride". They hooked him on to a cable behind a personnel carrier and dragged him along. They delighted in taking their vengeance.

When they went into houses, they killed everybody. They crapped on the carpets and drank pure alcohol from the crystal vases. All the valuable items went to the senior officers, who sent them back home to Russia.

Maxim couldn't remember why he killed the old woman. He'd probably been really high on grass.

"Pardon me for interrupting," said Maxim, draining his glass in a single gulp. "I'll just be a moment."

Leaning on his stick, he cautiously made his way round the dancers and limped off in the direction of the toilet. What a good thing it was that alcohol dulled the pain in his leg. He stuck his head under the tap. Damnation! Why did he drink? The doctor had categorically forbidden him to drink.

They used to fire sometimes at night, but everyone had got used to it and they slept soundly. Apart from Maxim. He could clearly hear the resounding cries: "A-a-a-lla-a-ah A-a-akba-a-ar!"

The sound made the blood run cold in his veins. They'll kill us all here. Or slit our throats like sheep. Where are all those wonderful planes and the artillery you're so proud of, you bastards? We can't even get a mouthful of fresh air or take a smoke because of the sniper.

"A-a-a-lla-a-ah A-a-akba-a-ar!" the night cried out plaintively, again and again.

"Where's your heart now, Max? Sunk into your boots?" a sudden whisper asked in the darkness.

"No, higher than that, brother. Up my arse."

As he squeezed his way through between the smug, drunken faces veiled in clouds of tobacco smoke, Max realised that his beloved "Lily of the Valley" was not what it used to be. The discotheque, the long-legged waitresses, the meaningless clamour and hubbub had squeezed out the old, cosy, respectable atmosphere of the establishment. Just what was it that had happened to people while he'd been away? Why were they all laughing? What were they so happy about?

As he approached the table, he saw a strange man leaning down over Lizka.

"Aha! Here's your boyfriend." The stranger was swaying slightly and his manner was insultingly familiar. "You don't mind if I have a dance with your lady, do you?"

"I already told you I don't dance," said Lizka. She wanted to finish telling Max her funny story.

"Oh, don't say that, are you just going to sit here with your invalid? Don't be so stubborn!" The man made to reach out for Lizka, but Max managed to grab hold of his hand first.

"Listen, friend, better make it some other time."

"Get your hand off me, you cripple," the man said loudly and pushed Max away.

The group at the next table, to which the importunate guest evidently belonged, were following what was happening intently.

"Calm down, will you, both of you!" said Lizka, jumping to her feet. She had a bad feeling about all this.

"Why don't we go outside?" the man said, looking Max up and down contemptuously.

Max glanced at the next table.

"There's an entire gang of you. Why bother going outside? Let's do it here." And he punched the man hard on the bridge of his nose. The man howled and grabbed hold of his own face, and his friends jumped up from their table.

The attackers kept shouting something and jumping round Max, but he stood his ground confidently, wielding his stick. He struck deftly and precisely – at the Adam's apple, the crotch, the stomach. Someone jumped on him from behind and they both fell on the floor, taking the table down with them. As women shrieked and dishes broke Lizka was just thinking about how she'd ended up in trouble yet again, when Max grabbed her hand and dragged her towards the exit.

"Let's run for it!"

They skipped out into the street and Max pushed Lizka into the nearest alley.

"This damned leg!"

"You're crazy!" said Lizka, trying to break away from him.

"Sssssh!" Max led her in deeper, into the darkness of the courtyard.

They hid in a doorway and listened carefully to the voices and tramping feet of their pursuers.

"You're a crazy fool!" Lizka whispered angrily.

"And you're a thief," Max whispered back to her.

"What?" Lizka hissed, thinking the young guy really must be insane.

Max pointed downward, and Lizka saw a bottle of cognac in her hand. She could have sworn it had got there without her knowing anything about it.

A police siren howled somewhere, and then everything fell silent.

The night was spent in stormy, impetuous embraces and unrestrained passion in a room in the workers' hostel of the mechanical engineering plant, where Max operated a milling machine.

seven

IN THE MORNING Lizka went straight to work from Max's place, and she couldn't stop worrying about how Artur would react to the fact that she hadn't come home last night. Liubasha had already agreed to confirm that Lizka had been at her place. However, when they met at the trolleybus depot, Artur was astonishingly pleasant and polite.

"How are things?"

"All right."

"You don't need to go to the shop today, I'll buy everything myself."

"Okay," Lizka replied, surprised that he hadn't asked any questions.

They both lit up without saying anything.

"Maybe we could get away for a picnic on Wednesday?" Artur suggested.

"I can't on Wednesday, I've got a party with some of my girlfriends."

This was so unlike his usual way of behaving that Lizka started wondering if he'd spent the night at home himself. She remembered that there was supposed to be football on the TV the day before and decided to check.

"So who won? Spartak?"

"Since when have you been interested in football?"

"I just asked. Okay, it's time I was going!" Then she turned her back to her husband and shouted in a happy voice: "Liubasha, let's get cracking!"

As light green trolleybus number 17 set out on its route, Lizka was in an excellent mood. Her lecherous tomcat had either glutted himself on cream and now he was licking his lips, or he was feeling frightened because she could spend a night away from home too. The second option suited Lizka better. There was a feeling of guilt for being unfaithful trembling faintly somewhere deep in her soul, but it had been swamped immediately by a sense of satisfied vengeance and the mystery of a new, forbidden liaison. Compared with Artur, Max was a wild beast and a real man, not some kind of mummy's boy, but at the same he was dangerous because his insane destructive urge was so powerful. He attracted her, but she wouldn't have wanted to tie her life to a man like that, not for anything in the world. And then, although Artur would never show it openly, he really did love her. It was just that for some reason people hid their kindness, love and beauty somewhere deep inside. He loved her and they needed each other. And the idea of a picnic wasn't such a bad one bad, either. Perhaps she really ought to spend the last few sunny days out in the country? In early November the first snow would fall, then the frost would set in, and that would be the start of the six-month Russian winter – that season so loathsome to the soul and the body. Maybe she ought to pull out of the party and go out into the forest with her husband?

Her train of thought was interrupted by the sight of a familiar figure on the pavement. There weren't any stops here, but Lizka braked, opened the front doors and shouted: "Nina, jump in quick!"

Nina turned round and jumped into the tram as it was still moving, smiled with her sad eyes and muttered: "I'm not a stunt-woman, you know!"

She told Lizka that her architect's grandmother had died at last, only she hadn't left the apartment to him, but to some distant relative from another city. Now Nina was afraid that the lousy, rotten hostel would be her home for the rest of her life. Lizka tried to console her friend a little and distract her from her sad thoughts by inviting her to the hen party. Nina got out at her venereological clinic, waved her hand feebly in farewell and walked on, hunched over in an odd sort of way.

At the turning circle, when the girls were eating their lunch, Lizka was called to the controller's office for a phone call.

"Hello?"

"Hello, Liza? This is Max. I'm in militia station number 9. Can you get me out of here?"

"What's happened?"

"Nothing to worry about. So, will you collect me?"

"I have to work. I won't be free until three."

"I'll wait. Come then."

"All right," said Liza, without any real idea of why she was doing it.

For the rest of the working day Lizka was tormented by very unpleasant thoughts. Through militia channels it was no problem at all to trace a man with a limp who walked with a stick. Of course, they'd found him and now most likely they were going to charge him in connection with the fight in the "Lily of the Valley". But who would she be – an accomplice or a witness? And apart from that, she'd run away without paying, and she'd stolen a bottle of cognac. Damn it, maybe it would be better if she didn't go to the militia station at all?

And what if Max had really maimed someone? Or even killed them? He'd fought really savagely. All this could have absolutely terrible consequences, and the thought made Lizka feel really unwell. But then on Karl Marx Street fate gave her a little present.

Lizka spotted Hobgoblin in the passenger compartment. She hadn't changed much: she had the same hostile eyes behind those large spectacles, but the tip of her nose had got sharper – no doubt malice had sharpened it. Lizka felt like trapping her in the doors, but she was afraid of harming the other passengers. When Lizka saw that Hobgoblin was about to get off, she didn't drive up to the pavement, but stopped beside a large puddle instead.

"Outrageous!" the head of department exclaimed indignantly and set off for the other doors.

But the other doors slammed shut in her face. Lizka's voice announced the next stop and Hobgoblin had to get out through the only doors that were open, splashing disdainfully through the puddle. Lizka was triumphant. Let Hobgoblin write as many complaints to Lizka's bosses as she liked, after all, she didn't get that kind of opportunity every day!

Militia station number 9 had a strong smell of tobacco and male sweat and it was also very crowded. When Lizka's turn came in the queue for the little window into the duty office, she suddenly realised she didn't know Max's surname.

"I've come to collect my friend. He's called Max and he…" Lizka was very agitated.

"A ten-rouble fine," the duty officer said calmly.

Lizka rummaged in her handbag and handed him the money.

"And tell your friend that next time we'll put him away in solitary for two weeks. That's the last warning." Then the duty officer nodded to the colleague sitting beside him. "Let Shmyrin out."

There a rasping of metal somewhere and then Max appeared in front of Lizka, with a smile on his face. The sleeve of his jacket was torn and drops of blood had dried on to his split eyebrow.

"What happened? Did they pick you up because of what happened yesterday in the 'Lily of the Valley'?"

"No. I got bit rowdy in a different dive today. I punched this guy in the face and broke a couple of glasses." Max tried to kiss her, but his breath reeked of stale alcohol. Lizka turned away.

"Nothing to worry about," he said, without letting go of Lizka's hand, and led her towards the door. "The cops were impressed by my army papers and they forgave me, so the fine is just for being drunk."

"Listen, we have to talk," said Lizka, pointing to a bench outside the next building. "Let's sit down."

They sat down and lit up. Lizka looked into Max's eyes; they looked glazed and drunk, but there was a terrifying, obscure gleam of wild joy in them.

"You're a good guy, Max," she began timidly, "but I don't think it's a good idea for us to see each other. I have a husband I love and yesterday I was simply drunk and didn't know what I was doing."

"So what makes him any better than me?" Max asked in a quiet voice.

"It's not a question of who's better or worse. He's my husband, we're a family."

"It's because of my leg, isn't it? You don't want to get involved with a cripple?"

"It's got nothing to do your leg. That can be cured eventually, anyway."

"It's not very likely. The joint's damaged, you can't just stick in a metal tube. I'm never likely to earn enough for an artificial limb, and

all I get from the state is a three-rouble greetings card every year for
the Day of Defenders of the Fatherland."

"I'm very sorry, Max, but I can't be with you. I don't love you."

"Maybe you could come to love me?" said Max, putting his hand
on Lizka's knee.

"Oh, good God, no!" She jumped up and walked away quickly.
"No! And don't call me any more."

After this not very pleasant meeting, Lizka thought what big
children men really are and how easily they pretend to be hard
of hearing when it suits them. Lizka had certainly been flattered
by Max's interest, but today's escapade had finally convinced her
that their relationship was impossible. Lizka wanted to live with
someone who was creative, not destructive, and she remembered
Victor Mikhailovich. Where was he now? She'd heard that many of
the old Party and Komsomol leaders had been left unemployed or
were getting by working as schoolteachers. Apart from governing
other people, they didn't know how to do anything at all. According
to the newspapers, even the First Secretary of the Communist Party
of G. was working as a night watchman in some warehouse. If she
happened to see Victor in her trolleybus now, she'd definitely take
the opportunity to go up to him and say how good it was that his
kind had been rejected.

To her great surprise, Victor Mikhailovich popped up that very
evening. As she and Artur were eating dinner in front of the television,
she heard a familiar voice and saw Victor's face, which hadn't changed
at all. He was standing on a stage, surrounded by flashing cameras and
explaining his platform for the elections coming up in December. As
dashing and energetic as ever, and very convincing, he was standing
to be governor of G., and the analysts were already predicting that he
would win forty-two per cent of the votes.

"Yes," Artur sighed and switched over to a different channel. "It looks like there's nothing changing up there on top. If it carries on like this, we'll never earn enough for an apartment, or get new trolleybuses, and those hormone tablets of yours will just go on lying untouched in the cupboard. It's a completely hopeless situation."

"What's the point in whining, why don't you think of something?" Lizka objected.

"Are you suggesting I ought to become a gangster or a speculator?"

"Not necessarily. Other people manage to live and get rich too," Lizka replied, and she repeated Yeltsin's phrase: "Now is the time of opportunities."

"Yes, but for who? Do you remember Danila, the chairman of our trade union?"

"Uh-huh."

"Well, now he's got five kiosks spread right across the city: beer, cigarettes, all sorts of bits and pieces. So, in one of the five he decided to do everything according to the law, as an experiment, so to speak. Not only has that kiosk not earned him a single kopeck for more than three months, Danila actually still owes the state money. A fine for filling out his tax returns incorrectly!"

"And so you intend to spend your entire life lying on the sofa in front of the television? We've got to do something."

"I know what we need to do. I've got this grandiose plan for the entire country," said Artur, with a cunning expression in his eyes. "We have to take huge loans from the West again, and then use the money to hire our own creditors to write laws that make sense, put the economy in order and pay off the debt that we owe them. That's the best plan for the future of Russia!"

Lizka suddenly felt sad. Instead of thinking about her and their future child, he always fobbed her off with some stupid joke or other. But she didn't argue or object, she just snuggled in under his arm and said: "Let's go to bed."

"No, don't be silly. The football's on in ten minutes."

The long-anticipated hen party on Wednesday began at ten in the morning. The girls already started drinking while they were making the snacks, because the next morning they all had to start driving again. And since the medical test was very strict, they always invited the doctor, Zoya Andreevna, to cover themselves. Because of her job, the fat, flabby, red-nosed doctor took part in all of the trolleybus depot's drinking parties. She was a poor conversationalist, but she was magnificent at braising meat. Nina and Lizka chopped the salads, Liubasha and Lizka's partner Katya laid the table, while Vera looked through the old records and boasted to her conductor Irina about the new car she'd just got.

"A 1989 Passat, neatly stolen in Germany and repainted! I'll keep it running for another twenty years, and after another layer of paint it will look as pretty as a picture. We'll get drunk now, and then, when it gets dark, we'll go for a drive and pick up some lovely boys or, better still, girls. There's lots of space, everyone will fit in!"

The rather mannish Vera made no secret of her predilection for the female sex. She had a pragmatic view of the world and was respected at the depot for her love of technology. Unlike the other women drivers, she didn't decorate her cabin with flowers, glittery knick-knacks and pretty curtains, she was more concerned about the pressure in the tyres, the clutch and, above all, the sound of the engine. And since she never trusted the welders and mechanics, and enthusiastically did everything herself, her trolleybus was rarely off the road for repairs and, despite its age, it was probably the most reliable in the entire depot.

She and her husband, who worked in a car showroom that sold foreign makes, had not come together out of love at all, but out of common interests. He was a secret homosexual who regarded sex as a sport that required technique and stamina, and all in all he suited Vera rather well. She raised his child, and in gratitude for that, he bought her cars. They rarely poked their noses into each other's business, but just for fun they competed to see who could seduce the most straights. Her conductress Irina, who had married a man twice her own age when she was just seventeen, and was still cursing herself for it, admired Vera, but she wouldn't let her come near her, despite all the stubborn rumours circulating at the depot that they were lovers.

Lizka and Katya serviced their light green number 17 trolleybus in a rather haphazard fashion, so they couldn't boast of its impeccable performance. All they could do was envy Vera's skill and sigh: "This bus has been cursed for all eternity! There's no way we can do anything with it!"

"You're fools, girls! A trolleybus has a soul too, you just can't understand it," Vera laughed at them. "What's happened this time?"

"The handrail's fallen off again," Katya complained pitifully. "It always falls off during my shift."

It wasn't clear whether this ill-starred trolleybus had a soul or not, but the handrail on the rear platform definitely had one. It wouldn't accept bolts or even welding and it was constantly hitting unsuspecting passengers on the head or dumping the poor unfortunates on the dirty floor. Its favourite times were during bends in the road and the crush at the stop in front of the Mikhailovsky market, and it regarded bad winter weather, when the floor of the passenger compartment was a liquid slurry of sand and snow, as the most suitable period for its attacks on the public.

"Bloody hell!" all the passengers would exclaim in unison, and all fall over sideways together, clutching the detached handrail like a spear that mutilated the faces and clothes of the people standing in front of them.

Lizka quarrelled with the welders; Katya hung a sign on the handrail: "DO NOT TOUCH!", but nothing helped. Lizka and Katya were afraid even to talk about the other defects of their vehicle, in case they jinxed it, and because they didn't want to cast a shadow over the happy feast.

From trolleybuses the conversation naturally turned to money. They remembered last year's strike: their competitors from trolleybus depot number 2 had ignored it and worked as normal, and the director of their trolleybus depot had punished his striking drivers by docking their wages and taking away their bonuses. They had moaned about the lack of unity, they had brought up the examples of the French long-distance lorry drivers and the Israeli teachers, but everything had stayed just the same – and their miserly wages were paid four months late.

That only made them all the more admiring and envious of Katya, who managed to dress like a queen, thanks to her sewing machine. Long raincoats, hats with wide brims, exotic dresses – everything she could use to avoid giving away her profession. She had even managed to find spectacles with plain lenses from somewhere, to make her look more like a librarian than a trolleybus driver. The others took their example from her, and so the next two hours were devoted to studying fashion magazines. Lizka, who wore anything that would do, thought this was a pointless exercise. What sense did it make to iron a skirt, if you had to carry it around in a plastic bag all day long because there weren't any changing-rooms? Better wear a tracksuit and leather jacket. She started feeling bored and walked over to the window.

The day had turned out cloudy, and there weren't many people in the courtyard. Vera's dark green Passat really did look brand, sparkling new, and it stood out among the other parked cars. Not far away from it, there was a man leaning against a birch tree and smoking. Oh God, no! It was Max. Lizka hastily moved away from the window, and thoughts started running feverishly through her head. How did he know that she was here? Was it a coincidence? Was he following her? She felt afraid.

"Vera, will you give me a lift home today?"

"No problem," Vera mumbled curtly and turned her face back to Katya's finger, which was running over another pattern, accompanied by practical advice from its owner.

Lizka calmed down a bit and glanced out of the window again. There was no one under the birch tree. Perhaps she'd simply imagined it was Max?

"My nerves are shot to pieces!" she said, angry with herself, and drained her glass in a single gulp.

"But I protest!" Irina exclaimed with a hiccup. She was still young and didn't know how to hold her drink yet, and she was already very tipsy. "Why do we have to dress like these dolls in the magazines? Let's dress to suit our wages, or anyone might think we're happy with this shitty life! Making ourselves out to look like ladies, and at home the walls are bare and there's nothing to feed the kids with!"

"Do you want to frighten away the fellers?" Liubasha objected. "There's nothing but alcoholics left as it is."

"Just because your ex drank like a fish, it doesn't mean they're all like that," Zoya Andreevna put in.

That brought up the second subject – men, who were held responsible for all the miseries of women. The discussion essentially came down to dividing all men into three categories. The first category was bastards and scumbags and it included, above all, their colleagues the male trolleybus drivers and all male drivers in general. The second category included spongers or dictators who were former or present husbands and lovers, who had lazed around and oppressed their women, suddenly lost interest in them and generally disappointed their delicate, defenceless female inner beings. The third category was supposed to be for kind, decent, affectionate men who were also strong and self-confident, but it turned out that no one there had met anyone like that yet.

The girls were always glad when they reached conclusions like that, and their hearts were filled with a feeling of solidarity. The disagreements, if there had been any, faded away, envy and malice evaporated, and Zoya Andreevna would start singing her favourite song:

True lovers never renounce their love

The others would immediately take it up and put their souls into singing it, with their eyes closed.

For life does not end tomorrow,
I shall stop waiting for you,
But you will come quite unexpectedly
True lovers never renounce their love

And you will come when it is dark,
When the blizzard rattles the window,

When you recall how long it is
Since we have warmed each other,
Yes, you will come when it is dark.

Lizka looked at Nina, who had tears pouring down her cheeks. Nina's voice began to tremble, and she stopped singing, in order not to spoil the harmony. And in order not to let the others see this weakness of hers, she opened a bottle and poured wine for everyone.

And you will want so much
The warmth you did not love before.
The queue of three for the phone,
Will be too much for you to endure,
You will want that warmth so much.

For this it is worth giving everything.
I believe in it so much,
It is hard for me not to wait for you
All day, standing by the door,
For this it is worth giving everything.

After the first song they had another drink, wiped away the tears, blew their noses and started a second. How little a woman really needs to be happy, thought Lizka. She wanted to go back home right now, go home to Artur and just press herself against him or throw him on the bed and take him by force, just as long as he didn't say anything.

But as the songs and the bottles flew by and the evening advanced, the intimate, personal themes gave way to noisy, riotous socialising. They said goodbye to hospitable Liubasha and saw Nina on her way – she had to start the night shift. And then the Passat full of drunken girls went flying round the streets of the city to take all the others home. And despite Vera's dubious jibes, Lizka finally managed to persuade her friend to let her drive.

"Ah, how little everything is!" she laughed. "And how low!"

"Lizka, not so fast! Please, be more careful," Zoya Andreevna gasped.

"Don't worry, girls! Talent isn't a rouble, you can't just drink it away!"

Lizka found the familiar potholes seen from an unfamiliar angle very amusing, and the automobile's manoeuvrability and the sensitivity of the tiny steering wheel delighted her so much that she felt like squealing.

"Tell me, Vera, do you think your husband could give me a toy like this as a present?"

But Vera wasn't listening to her. Vera, Irina and Katya had wound down the windows and were amusing themselves by hailing the people walking or driving by, shouting something or other and waving their hands about excitedly. A black BMW drew level with them, and then the driver politely decided not to overtake.

"Hey, handsome, I want you!" Irina shouted to him. "Where are you going?"

Meanwhile the BMW settled back into their lane and blinked its headlamps twice, as if it was trying to tell them something.

"Damn, there's the fuzz!"

About two hundred metres ahead of them a dark bend in the road was illuminated by a light blinking red and blue.

"Shall I stop?"

"And lose your licence and your job?" Vera shouted. "Let me in there!"

The traffic police Moskvich had already moved out into the roadway and was rapidly gaining on them. Lizka turned the wheel sharply, cutting across the opposite lane of traffic and down a short side-street, and found herself on a parallel street.

"Girls, let me out of here," Zoya Andreevna wailed pitifully.

"Shut up!" barked Katya. "We can get into the Ivanovsky Park here! Turn left down Samarkand Lane!"

Lizka's heart was pounding furiously. She let two cars go by, then went flying out on to the next parallel street and swung sharp left. The car skipped over the curb, sending everyone bouncing up to the ceiling and just missing a park bench by some miracle, then shot in behind the bushes under the sheltering darkness of the trees.

"Everybody keep quiet!" Katya said, and leaned over Lizka's shoulder to switch off the ignition.

"Lizka, I'll kill you!" Vera whispered

The militia Moskvich appeared from the other side of the park, stood there in bewilderment for about thirty seconds, then went dashing off, with its siren wailing through the night air.

"I personally think it's a matter of honour, because we're better than all these machos," said Irina, breaking the silence. "So what are we doing now, hiding from that handsome guy in the BMW?"

They smoked in silence for few minutes. Then Zoya Andreevna and Katya took Irina under the arms and staggered off with her to the nearest bus stop. Vera began showering Lizka with reproaches and swore never to trust her with her car again. Lizka defended herself, claiming that if it wasn't for her, everything could have turned out far worse. But when she didn't find any visible signs of damage, Vera calmed down a bit, although she did mutter something about a crack in the side frame. When they'd cooled down and made up, they left the car in the nearest car park, so as not to tempt fate a second time and decided to celebrate a generally successful end to the evening in some bar.

There, surrounded by bronze neon-lit faces, tables and glasses, Lizka chewed on sugary segments of lemon with her vodka, and told Vera about Artur and Maxim: she said she was about just about ready to explode, that when she was a child, she'd imagined life would be quite different – not so contradictory and even senseless. And in her opinion children ought to have the right to choose whether to be born into a world like this or not. Lizka herself was going to spare her children the pain. And as well as that, she declared, she was pursued by cruel bad luck, and that was the simple explanation for what had happened today. The malicious outside world, with its injustice and cruelty, had already completely crushed every last grain of hope and faith she'd ever had in everything bright and good, and poverty had strangled her spiritual side, so that any harmony between her soul and her body had become impossible.

"…this damn blasted nonsense all the time! The tyre on the rear left wheel has started leaking badly again, and I'm so pissed off with having to pump it up twice a day! How's that going to generate large earnings, and high wages to match? The last time I went to the theatre was with the rest of my class, when I was still at school!" Liza said in conclusion of her monologue.

Vera stroked Lizka's hand, followed the movements of her lips with an intoxicated gleam in her eyes and tried to reassure her. She advised Lizka not to think of the world as something external and hostile and to stop thinking of herself as the centre of a universe that had to revolve around her – which was the mistake that most people made – but come to terms with it and accept that we are all only insignificant little parts of a whole that is still unknown. She said that the difference between good and bad is a very relative business, and you have to learn to value the beautiful moments of happiness on the way along a road as short as the life that God has granted us. As she poured more for Lizka than for herself, Vera declared that an opinion about something is not the same as the thing itself, just as, for instance, the anticipation of a celebration is more enjoyable than the celebration itself, and the anticipation of death is more frightening than death itself. Vera said all sorts of other wise things as well, and Lizka didn't entirely understand what she was saying and why, but she was very impressed by her friend anyway. And when the bottle was empty, Vera finally suggested that Lizka should stay the night with her, as she only lived two blocks away.

They both got into the same bed for the night. One with timid curiosity, the other with impatient passion.

On Thursday a roadside pillar collapsed on the Street of the Electricians. It happened in the early hours, before dawn, for reasons that were completely incomprehensible. The immense reinforced concrete structure, crowned by a streetlamp and carrying dozens of different types of cables, lay across the roadway, blocking it and causing a traffic jam almost a kilometre long. The power was cut off for eight trolleybuses from depot number 4, so they had to let off their disgruntled passengers, lower their booms and dolefully form up in a column. Some of the drivers got out for a smoke, others wiped down their headlights and windscreens, and others, for lack of anything better to do, went off to watch the repair team at work. Liubasha was dozing on her conductor's seat with an open book in her hands. Sometimes her head would jerk up in response to some sound, and Liubasha would try to concentrate on her reading, but she immediately started nodding off again and her eyelids gently closed. Lizka was smoking in her cabin, staring blankly at some point on the rear bumper of the trolleybus standing in front and imagining the conversation she was going to have with her husband. She wanted to tell him that she had got confused and tired, that they needed to try to start all over again, to be more sensitive and support each other more. But what she was afraid of was that he'd avoid a conversation like that or simply turn it into another joke. She was so sick of his feeble humour!

At the same time she was suffering from a hangover, belated fright following the previous day's escapade in the car and – even worse than that – embarrassment at her memories of the night spent with Vera. Lizka couldn't have said she didn't enjoy the night, but she was tormented by a sense of irredeemable sin that hadn't left her since she had first opened her eyes that morning and seen Vera's ear on the pillow beside her. They had maintained an awkward silence while they drank coffee and walked to work together. Lizka didn't know how to behave with Vera now. And just as she began thinking about her, there she was, knocking on the window.

"Looks like we're stuck here for the whole day. I'm up in front of you, three buses along. Have you got a key for number 17?"

"Here," Lizka wound down the window and handed her the key.

"Maybe we could have dinner together today?" Vera asked very directly.

"No. You know, I…"

"Okay, don't worry about it. I was only joking," Vera said with a smile and set off back to her trolleybus.

As Lizka watched her go, an unpleasant thought occurred to her: what if Vera boasted about her lesbian exploits at the depot and told everyone she'd slept with Lizka? Her cheeks flushed bright red. Unable to drive away these depressing thoughts, which were reinforced by her hangover, Lizka got out into the street and also went to watch the workmen in bright red vests clearing away the collapsed pillar with a crane. They were going about it very nervously, with more hand-waving and swearing than any clear understanding of the job in hand. It was clear now to everyone that the working day was over and the trolleybuses would have to be left here for the night. She just wanted to get home as soon as possible.

Artur spent the next two nights away from home, but Lizka wasn't too worried – she thought he was simply getting his own back on her. She didn't have her conversation with him until Saturday, after work. They sat down facing each other and Lizka just couldn't make up her mind where to start. Artur seemed far too severe this time around, and his whole manner suggested that he had something on his mind too.

"I'm leaving you," he said at last, and turned his eyes away.

"What do you mean?" Liska asked, taken aback.

"I don't love you any more and I want to apply for a divorce." The words sounded so definite, so confident that Lizka started violently.

She hadn't been expecting this turn of events at all: she understood his words, but she didn't want to accept what they meant.

"Artur, how can you? We're husband and wife…"

"I'm going to live with Katya, your partner," Artur interrupted in a calm voice. "It's all decided and there's nothing to discuss. We've been seeing each other for two months already."

Lizka felt overwhelming pain, indignation and fury. The indignation shattered against the cold glance of this man so dear to her, leaving a bitter taste in her throat and the indignation burst out in a wild shout.

"Katya! That bitch? Everyone in the depot sleeps with her! And apart from that, she's got a child."

"That doesn't concern you." Artur was still calm, but obviously sensing that he was hurting Lizka, he softened his voice. "I'm leaving you this room and moving in with her."

Lizka was shattered. How could her friend and partner act this way? And then – she, Lizka, had the right to leave someone, but no one had any right to leave her. Throughout a sleepless night she asked herself why it hurt her so much to lose Artur. Perhaps their love had simply been replaced by habit and the appearance of stability, and she found these hard to give up? Or perhaps it had only been the illusion of love, if she didn't feel any desire to keep him beside her or fight for him? But those words of his: "I'm leaving you" had sounded so calm and simple. Did a surgeon really tell his patient so calmly and indifferently that he was going to cut his arm off?

On Sunday Max phoned the turning circle and begged Lizka to see him in a drunk, agitated voice.

"Will you leave me in peace, for God's sake! I don't want any men, or women! I want to be alone! I'm going to buy myself a dog!" she shrieked down the phone and hung up.

EIGHT

TWO WEEKS OF unpaid leave did Lizka a lot of good. She was glad not to have to get up for work, not to have to see Katya and Artur and listen to her colleagues gossiping behind her back. She took herself in hand, went to the hairdresser's and bought a few clothes, calculating that if she ate nothing but apples and yoghurt, her money would last until the next pay day. Lizka even tried to learn Wushu from a self-instruction manual, but after the very first lesson her muscles began aching so badly that she switched to reading fantasy novels instead. In the evenings, she went round the bars with Nina and Vera, but she only drank orange juice, afraid that if she drank alcohol she'd only end up in some mess or other.

"Try to answer this question for yourself: are you going to be something all your life, instead of someone? If you think that happiness can be built around a man, you're mistaken. In eighty years of Soviet power they've completely forgotten how to work, and I wouldn't put any trust in those idle, useless bumpkins," Vera preached to Lizka, taking a long swig of beer and a drag on her cigarette. "And what kind of way is that to behave, getting married at the drop of a hat? There are thousands of women who live on their own and take lovers and then change them."

"And you think they're happy?" Nina interrupted her.

"Perfectly! If you think about it, these men cause more harm than good. Either they get jealous without any reason, or they get these crazy whims that you have to follow, like a dumb fool, and all your attention has to be devoted to them, and then there's all that housework. But if you're on your own, when you feel like it you can cook yourself something tasty, and if you don't feel like it, you can treat yourself at the cake shop. No need to tidy up the flat right now if you don't feel like it, do it the day after tomorrow or even next week. So I advise you both to make yourselves financially independent, and give up men."

"What, completely?" asked Nina.

"No, why completely?" Vera exploded. "Go down to the discotheque, pick up some nice-looking stud, sleep with him and go your separate ways – no problems. There are plenty of other interesting things in life, aren't there?"

"It's all too simple the way you put it," Nina objected. "What you suggest is just to live for yourself, to soar like a butterfly while you're still young. What about when you get old? The loneliness? No family, no grandchildren. Then you start asking: why was I put in this world, what did I live for, if I couldn't even be a mother? I know those kind of women very well. If a lady's approaching forty and she lives with a cat or a dog, then she's either an old maid or a lesbian."

Vera was a little offended by this, but she immediately recovered and replied: "What's that got to do with it? It doesn't take brains to make children, and you can raise a child on your own as well."

"But the sons of single mothers grow up to be mummy's boys or gays, and their daughters turn out like that…" Nina cast an oddly maternal glance at Lizka, who was eating pilaff with an apathetic air.

Holding her little finger out to one side, she was trying to pick up the rice on her fork, but it kept scattering and wouldn't go into her mouth. Nina finally couldn't stand it any more – she went over to the bar counter, came back with a spoon and stuck it in Lizka's hand.

"There. Make it easy on yourself."

"Tell me, Nina, where did you get this habit of generalising everything?" Vera persisted.

"I don't generalise, I just say what I think. And apart from that, I'm not a feminist or a lesbian."

"What are you trying to say?"

"Nothing, it's just that, unlike you, I like men."

"That's right, because you're a primitive animal."

"That's enough, girls, stop it!" It seemed to Lizka that her friends were on the point of quarrelling, and so she decided to change the subject. "Maybe we should all change our jobs? Why don't all three of us go into trade? We'll go on trips to Turkey and China, buy clothes there wholesale, and then sell them in the market here or, even better, in our own shop."

"First tell me where you're going to get your starting capital!" Vera said caustically.

"A bank loan."

"Ha! Are you going to show them proof of your earnings?"

"Then we'll sell your Passat."

"And why not the wheels off your trolleybus?"

At this point the girls were overcome by the kind of laughter that's just impossible to resist. They imagined themselves bribing the depot watchman Kolya with a bottle of vodka and then unbolting the huge wheels that were almost as tall as they were. Their laughter was a mixture of their common concerns, a feeling of hopelessness and the total absurdity of the situation each of them was in. They doubled over in laughter, sometimes shooting short glances at each

other, only to burst into a new peal a moment later. The customers
in the bar turned their heads to look at them in annoyance, or trying
to guess the reason for this merriment. But there are either too many
reasons for that kind of laughter, or only the people laughing know
them. Nina was probably laughing at her vain hopes of moving
into her architect's grandmother's apartment. Vera could have been
laughing, for instance, at the fact that Interpol could confiscate her
car at any time. And as for Lizka, she was laughing because her
friends were laughing, and also because just at that moment she
could stop thinking about Artur. She didn't want any more of this
self-pity, these harmful comparisons with the people around her,
these destructive thoughts about divorce. She didn't have to buy him
meat anymore, she could buy expensive lipstick. And even if the
director of the trolleybus depot didn't grant her request and switch
her to the remote route number 25 and she stayed on route 17, then
neither Artur nor Katya would ever see how she was suffering. She
would be a beautiful, seductive flirt.

Nina was the first to calm down. Breathing heavily, she wiped
away the tears, took a gulp of beer and said: "I've just realised that
you're both hopelessly ill."

Vera and Lizka burst into laughter again.

"Yes, yes," Nina continued. "It's concealed schizophrenia, but
I'll cure you. Come to the flying club the day after tomorrow at six
o'clock in the evening and bring twenty dollars with you."

"I don't have twenty dollars," Lizka said quickly. "Vera, will you
lend me the money?"

"No problem."

When she found Max at the entrance to her house, Lizka felt confused
and frightened. It meant that he was following her after all, and now

he knew where she lived. This time he was carefully shaved, sober and holding a bouquet of chrysanthemums in his hand.

"Hello."

"Hello."

Lizka had no intention of inviting him into her home, and so there was nothing left for her to do but lower herself helplessly on to the steps of the entrance. Max handed her the flowers and sat down beside her.

"What do you want from me?" She asked the question as hostilely as she could, secretly hoping that the conversation would be short.

Max seemed to understand her tone of voice and her tired expression and so he came straight out with it: "Give me a chance."

"No."

"Perhaps…"

"No."

They said nothing for a while.

"Want a cigarette?"

"No. Why me in particular? There are plenty of other girls around."

"I want to see you, talk to you, I can't live without you."

"I don't need anyone. No one in this world needs anyone anyway. If I'm so important to you, give me your word that this is the last time we'll see each other."

"I can't," said Max, concealing a grimace of pain as he helped himself up with his stick, and walked away.

Lizka rejected the idea of reporting his pursuit of her to the militia, since she didn't wish him ill at all. She could only guess at what was going on inside his head, and she was afraid he might easily start a fight if they tried to arrest him.

Before, when she watched soldiers marching along the street, she used to admire their fine bearing and dress uniforms. She used to like the barely concealed smiles on those serious faces, and the greedy glances thrown at her skirt had sometimes felt flattering. There was something noble and romantic about the gleaming buttons and boots, and she felt proud that her father had been an officer. But recently more and more young guys like Max had appeared. Liubasha had once calculated that almost one passenger in ten travelled free as an army veteran. Border Guard Day and Paratrooper's Day more often than not ended in mass riots and clashes with the militia. There were helicopters on the television – and not the ones they were used to seeing over the city – and parents hid their sons to avoid them being conscripted into the army.

Lizka watched Max's back as he walked away, and she suddenly felt acutely sorry for him. And she might just have given him a chance, but not now, not after Artur had left.

That night Lizka had a nightmare: she was standing on some mud track in the middle of open countryside, and there was an entire herd of wild horses rushing straight at her. Because of the high grass, she couldn't see their legs, only their heads and manes. They were getting closer and closer, and if she didn't do something immediately, they would knock her down and trample her. She looked round, searching for somewhere safe to run to, and saw a trolleybus slowly drifting past her. She didn't understand how it could move without any power cables, but the door was open, offering her safety, and she dashed towards it. The leading stallion had already caught up with her and was galloping alongside. She could clearly see his big black eye looking sideways at her. There was something diabolical, insane and familiar in that eye. She looked closer and was horrified: it was Max. She was so frightened that she couldn't breathe, her legs went

numb, she couldn't run anymore and the trolleybus began leaving
her behind. The immense stallion's head with Max's eyes was trying
to knock her down on to the ground and laughing malevolently.

When she woke up, Lizka thought she ought to read less fantasy,
and just to be on the safe side she decided to stay at Liubasha's place
for a couple of days.

When Nina met her friends at the bus stop near the flying club, she
had a conspiratorial smile on her face.

"Did you bring the money?"

Vera and Lizka nodded.

"Then let's go, we don't have much time!"

She set off across a waste lot towards the tall wooden fence
crowned with barbed wire.

"Have you decided to have a picnic on the airfield, then, is that
it?" Vera asked.

"You'll find out everything soon enough. Get a move on, we've
only got ten minutes left." She stopped at the fence and moved two
boards aside to make a narrow gap. "Follow me!"

When they were on the other side, Nina pointed to a small,
rickety-looking plane standing in the distance and declared proudly:
"That's ours!"

"Brilliant!" Vera exclaimed and gave Nina a loud kiss on the
cheek.

"You're not going to fly in that, are you?" asked Lizka, feeling a
chill shudder run down her spine.

"Certainly I am!" said Nina, dragging her two friends in the
direction of the plane.

There were four young men sitting on the yellow grass under
the wing, waiting for them. One of them, obviously the leader,

kept looking nervously at his watch and only said hello after he'd counted the money.

"Let me introduce our instructor, Dima," Nina announced. "And this is his team: Vanya, Sergei and the pilot Kolya. How are you doing, boys?"

The young guys said hello, Dima looked the girls over critically, then took off his jacket and handed it to Vera.

"Take your coat off and put this on. Everything else is on board. After you." He opened the door and pulled down the steps.

"I've never flown before, I'm afraid," Lizka began, but Nina shoved her inside without even saying a word.

The girls sat on one of the benches along the sides, the young men seated themselves facing them and the instructor Dima began rummaging in the aluminium crates standing beside them.

"Will someone tell me at last what we're going to do?" Lizka asked, tugging at Nina's sleeve.

But Nina was too busy for her now, she'd got involved in a lively discussion with the young guys, who were sharing something, or somebody, out among themselves.

"Vera, who do you want to go with?"

"I'll go with Dima. No, better let him take Lizka."

"Then I'll take Vanya."

Lizka's vague suspicion was confirmed when the young men started putting on parachutes. Surely they weren't going to make her jump too! But they didn't give her a parachute, or her friends either, there were only three of them. That was it, of course, they were just going to watch Nina's friends jump. Lizka calmed down.

"Actually, the boss hasn't okayed any flights this week," the instructor Dima said, turning to Lizka and handing her a red helmet, "but anything for a friend. Here, put this on. You're jumping with me."

"What do you mean, I'm jumping?" asked Lizka, turning cold. "I don't know how. I won't…"

Her words were drowned out by the roar of the motor. Dima sat down beside her and fastened her belt, she caught a glimpse of birch trees through the small round windows and a moment later some unknown force tore them away up and away from the ground. The plane swayed from side to side; it seemed to Lizka that this unreliable device was about to fall and crash at any moment, and she began thinking that today she was going to die in a very stupid and absurd way, and all because of her friend's crazy whim, and she was still so young. The expressions on all the others' faces were calm and even joyful, and Lizka couldn't understand why these people were voluntarily putting themselves in danger. The plane heeled over on one side, setting the crates creeping across the floor.

"When we get out, do this," Dima said loudly into her ear, crossing his hands on his chest. "Don't wave your legs about and don't be afraid of anything."

Then the young men got up and each took a girl and stood her in front of him, with her back to him, and began fiddling about with some straps. The door into the pilot's cabin opened and the pilot Kolya waved his hand.

"It's time!"

Lizka was fastened tightly to Dima, and she could feel him pushing her towards the exit. She braced her legs against the floor with all her might, but the instructor turned out to be stronger, and her feet slid implacably towards the edge of the open door. The wind struck her in the face.

"Banzai!" Dima yelled in her ear.

"Mummy!" Lizka heard her own voice say, and then suddenly there was nothing under her feet.

Her breath was taken away, everything began spinning round her and she squeezed her eyes tight shut, feeling nothing but the blood pounding at her temples. There was a popping sound and the straps bit into her hips. Lizka felt herself soaring upwards and she opened her eyes. What she saw filled her with such delight that she couldn't help squealing out loud.

The squares of brown and yellow fields, divided by dark lines, extended all the way to the wavy foliage of the forest, with its bright autumn colours, with the summer house settlement looking like a huge patchwork blanket spread out beside it. Over to the right, the city was a fantastic mosaic of streets and roofs that stretched all the way to the horizon, with the golden domes of the churches glittering brightly in the sun at its centre. Cars like matchboxes crawled slowly across the toy bridge over the river, which from up there looked like a small stream winding down the inclined surface to somewhere in the far distance. Lizka had never thought before that a river could have an incline, but now she could make it out quite clearly. There were funny little insect-people crawling about on the intersecting ribbons of the streets.

"Look!" Dima shouted, and turned Lizka's head in the direction of his outstretched arm. "The first snow!"

There in the distance, where he was pointing, Lizka saw a white sheet that stood out sharply on a ploughed field. As she looked at its sharp outlines, Lizka was amused at the idea that over there this early, fluffy snow had already fallen, without any real breath of winter in it, and tomorrow it would melt, but there wasn't any snow here yet.

But now they were already very low, and the ground was

beginning to come up at them faster and faster. They could clearly see the warehouses and Industrial Street, the empty lot and the fence round the flying club. They rushed by above the tops of the fir trees so quickly that Lizka's eyes began to water, then there was an open field in front of them and the runway in the distance. And there was the pale, withered grass.

"Two steps, and we fall to the right, Dima said in her ear. "Like this."

Lizka's feet touched the ground and Dima pulled her down on to her side after him with a laugh and asked: "Well, how was it?"

"I want to do it again!"

While Dima freed her from her straps, Lizka watched the others land and, once she was free, she set off at a run towards Nina at the other side of the airfield. She saw Vera running towards Nina from the direction of the forest.

"It's fantastic! It's fantastic!" she shouted.

"Why didn't you tell me you go parachuting?" Lizka asked, grabbing hold of Nina's arm. "I want to do it again. I must do it again!"

"It's only the second time I've jumped myself. I only got to know Dima just recently; he was a patient in our clinic too."

"Nina, thank you," Vera panted, putting her arms round her friends. "My God, I was so frightened. But then I thought: let's go for it! Who knows what's down there? No, there's life going on down there. And then we started spinning round so fast…"

"It looks as if the guys have got problems!" said Nina, pointing to the parachutists, who were slowly peeling off their parachutes, while a man ran towards them, shaking his fist in the air and shouting something angrily. Dima noticed him and gestured to the girls to go over to the fence.

"My coat's still in the plane," Vera suddenly remembered.

"There'll be a reason to come back, then!" said Nina, heading for the hole in the fence. "Let's run for it!"

Once they'd escaped from the flying club's airfield, the girls went to a bar. They discussed the unusual event at length in excited voices and didn't go home until after midnight, in an unusually happy mood and feeling that they'd done something wonderful.

After her jump many things suddenly seemed unimportant to Lizka. For instance, her pitiful upstairs neighbour, the man who stuck his head out every time Lizka smoked by the window of her room and showered her with reproaches: "You're smoking there again! All the smoke comes up into my flat. My wife's crying already. If you don't stop, I shall be obliged to take stronger measures."

He said the same thing to her when they met by chance on the stairway or in the courtyard. Lizka advised him simply to close the window, or even complain to the municipal board of architects about the low ceilings, which made the windows so close to each other. She said there was no law forbidding anyone to smoke in their own home by an open window. But her neighbour wouldn't give up: he banged on the radiator and deliberately stamped his feet so that the old whitewash fell off her ceiling on to the floor. Lizka couldn't understand why this man had turned his life into a war with her. She imagined his shrew of a wife nudging him in the side and telling him in an almost hysterical voice: "Deal with that downstairs neighbour, will you! I don't want to breathe her tobacco smoke, but I'm not going to close my window just because of some smoker, either!"

Then Lizka remembered her parents, who had once rebuked her for carelessly brushing against the edge of a table and leaving a little scratch on the softwood parquet floor. Their indignation had astonished her so much that she'd begun to wonder whether things existed for people, or people existed for things.

How was it possible to live for such paltry goals, when there was the sky, the water, and then – the stars! And why hadn't she herself understood this before? And Lizka had wanted to shout out loud and tell all the people about it. Tell them to stop doing nothing but indulge their flesh and delight in life as it is here and now. This torrent of thoughts even made Lizka feel quite strange.

"What's happening to me?" she asked herself. "My God! I'm twenty-four already! I must be getting old."

And when Lizka sat at the wheel of her trolleybus again the next day, she smiled radiantly and felt unusually light; she felt like singing, she was in such a good mood. She took no notice of other people's rudeness and didn't snarl back at them the way she used to do before. When she drove out on to her route, she felt the same joy she had once felt when she made her first run on her own. Even though she was running behind schedule, Lizka waited for an old woman hurrying slowly towards the doors and all day long she let pedestrians across the road on the zebra crossings more often than usual. And she was also full of joy because she'd seen the first snow. That meant the autumn mud would soon be frozen solid by the frost, and then she'd be able to go outside in the new winter boots that had taken her almost six months to save up for.

During the lunch break Artur came up to her and asked how things were, adding that he was very sorry he'd been so rude and abrupt with her.

"Don't worry," she reassured him. "Things couldn't possibly be better!"

NINE

THAT WINTER WAS exceptionally severe: in the whole of January there was not a single day warmer than twenty degrees below freezing, and there was no more than one metre of snow. The call from my friend Andrei to tell me I absolutely had to come to the city of G. for an unofficial poets' forum caught me on the hop. Firstly, I had absolutely no money at all, and that meant I would have to hitchhike the entire six hundred kilometres. And in the middle of winter too! And secondly, this so-called forum was really nothing more than a week-long general binge, which was always held under the slogan: "The unpopular poet has one joy in life – a good booze-up with his friends!" The participants in this forum required great spiritual and physical strength, which I seriously doubted that I possessed, and in addition they were obliged to drink away their very last rouble and then make their way home, exhausted and unshaven, on anything that happened to be going their way. Gatherings like this were something like a consolation prize for those who had not managed to publish a single piece of their work all year long, and therefore for me too. Although I had made an effort.

To mark its fiftieth anniversary, the Red Metal-Worker mechanical engineering plant was intending to publish a miscellany of poems in praise of the achievements of labour, and its director had promised me a print-run of one thousand copies. In hopes of being able to publish my lyrical love poems, I had dedicated two of them with honest enthusiasm to the engineering plant – the first and the last. The director hadn't read the poems, and everything would have gone off brilliantly if the editor, a real pain in the neck, hadn't told him there was something here about "the moon and a woman's naked breast", thanks to which I was ignominiously shown the door.

The publishers who used to value poetry were all enthusiastically pursuing fantasy and detective novels, and were only prepared to publish poetry if the poet himself could find the money for it. And as for the senior editors of the local literary journals, they hadn't liked me for a long time already, because I just couldn't get into the spirit of national chauvinism. Their faces always look so intense and serious, you can't help thinking that with expressions like that they ought to be setting off for the trenches, or carrying a sledge hammer down a mine shaft. And then on top of that they ask: "And where's the educational element of militant patriotism in your writing? Surely you can see what a bad state the country's in?"

"And when was it ever in a good state?" I ask.

"No, you don't understand the task of literature, Instead of fighting against terrorism and encouraging a feeling of love for our Motherland, all your work is somehow negative, it completely lacks romanticism. What you need is a good beating to make you love Russia more."

"I already do love Russia. Only my Russia, not yours."

"You'd never know it from your poems."

"You don't know how to read them."

"And where are all the beautiful sights of your native parts, for instance? Where's all the suffering from unhappy love?"

"I don't want unhappy love, I'm for happy love…"

"That doesn't suit us. Goodbye!"

It's funny that even in poetry the muddle-headed former political officials continue to direct public opinion and decide for readers what they can read. It might be possible to understand these people, if only they didn't believe so fanatically in their own correctness. You can't get through to them with history, or any evidence of reality, or humour. Fanatics always drive you to despair. Maybe they're waiting for instructions from the capital? In short, thoughts like these had been making me feel sad, and so I told myself, as I usually did, "Why not?" and set out for G.

I already regretted putting on my high winter shoes instead of my felt boots when I was on the federal highway, just outside of town, which I had managed to reach by first taking a suburban train and then walking for a couple of kilometres. Skipping up and down and curling my toes tightly together in my shoes, I had been standing at the edge of the road in the clouds of powdered snow thrown up by all the trucks rushing by for more than an hour already. The frost was working its way deeper and deeper into me, but I was afraid of moving too energetically, in case I started to sweat. Every time a pair of headlights drew close, my hand flew up into the air hopefully, and every time it was lowered in disappointment as the red tail lights drove away, after which I hurled the most terrible of curses after the truck, hoping it would crash. Only one man stopped. He stuck his head out, looked me over from head to foot and asked indifferently: "Where to?"

"To G."

"How much are you paying?"

"If I had any money, I'd be sitting in a warm bus right now. But I can offer you a cassette of good music and I know a million jokes."

The driver didn't bother to answer me and drove on, having

given me just thirty seconds of warmth from his truck. "Russia has a generous soul," I thought, recalling the slogan from some advertisement. Generosity, compassion and altruism – these things don't exist here any more. Some other time I would probably have felt like pondering on the changes that my fellow-citizens had gone through in recent times, only not right there and right then, but in a soft armchair in a nice warm room.

It was getting light. The early-morning stream of trucks was over, now they passed by less often, and private cars had begun to appear. The people sitting in them gaped at me in astonishment as I hummed a tune to myself and danced a wild can-can. Some lady in a Volvo pointed me out to her passenger and twirled her finger in the air beside her temple.

"It would be more helpful if you stopped, you stupid fool," I shouted after her.

In my struggle with cold and despair such simple concepts as purpose and faith, things you hear about from other people and mention to them thousands of times, acquired a new meaning for me that day. I had already noted a haystack that I could bury myself in to hide from the wind, standing all alone under its snowy cap in the middle of a field, and a farm on the white horizon where I could probably also warm myself up a bit. I had lost the feeling in my toes and was already on the point of following one of these plans when a massive timber-carrier pulled up in front of me. Kazan number plates! I knew this one would take me.

The driver turned to be a jolly kind of man. I told him jokes, and he told me about bandits on the road – he'd seen plenty of them in all his years of working as a long-distance driver. His partner was sleeping on the bunk behind us.

A short cloudy day, the monotonous white ribbon of the road

in the headlights, a narrow patch of grey sky between the tops of the trees, the lights of some little village in the night, disappearing and then reappearing a hundred kilometres later, and impenetrable darkness – these were my companions on that winter journey. I arrived in the city of G. the next morning.

My friend Andrei greeted me with tea and cognac and expressed his regret that I had missed the previous evening but I, on the contrary was extremely glad that I had. From the experience of previous years, I knew that on the first evening all the poets spoke about nothing but themselves, only read their own poems and only listened to themselves. It was a thick blend of ambition, intrigue, jealousy, envy, narcissism and bragging, which under the influence of drink could even spill over into a fight. But now it was quiet, and all four rooms in Andrei's flat were cluttered with sleeping bodies. I recognised our veteran, Stepanych. The most elderly and most widely published lyric poet among us, Stepanych was in the habit of explaining to us callow youths that in his time water had been wetter and kilograms had been heavier. Andrei told me that Stepanych had been doing this with fervent passion the day before, and then he'd read some poems in his dramatic style, glaring in a wild, terrifying manner until the vodka had felled him. Now he was sleeping peaceably on the floor, calm and unassuming. I didn't try to identify the bodies of my other acquaintances, I just lay down myself, so that I would soon be able to glance into their honest, agonised, hung over...or, perhaps I should simply say their *genuine* eyes.

We drank for the whole week, without forgetting, naturally, to fill up our forums with discussions and papers. I especially liked the paper given by Igor, a poet from Perm, who asserted that it was impossible to write poetry with a straight face. You could deliver a baby with a straight face or disarm landmines with a straight face, but you couldn't make poetry. How well I agreed with him, remembering all those literary journal editors I detested! When the cognac and vodka ran out, we moved on to pure alcohol. Of course, some people might condemn us and recommend a more useful way of passing the time, but a poet needs a binge to clean out his own head, as a kind of disk defragmentation, because otherwise any poems begin to sound like total gibberish, including your own. Stepanych, for instance, tore one writer to shreds and accused him of violating the rules of versification and shameful amateurism. He carried on mocking the text of this author's poem for an hour, until he was told it was our country's national anthem.

On the last day of the forum a resolution was passed that consisted of two points. Firstly, we were pleased to acknowledge that although we were all idiots, none of us was alone. There were many of us. Secondly, we solemnly swore never again to consume *yorsh* made according to Andrei's recipe: six litres of beer and two litres of pure spirit mixed together in an enamel bucket.

I'm describing all this in such detail in order to give you a clear idea of the state we were in the next day. Andrei and I walked to the bus stop, carrying huge bags full of bottles in both hands, with our heads throbbing and our throats on fire, and the only thing both of us were thinking about was getting the empty bottles cashed in as soon as possible and buying a drink of cold beer with the money. The light green number 17 trolleybus was overcrowded, but we manage somehow to squeeze in through the front doors, with our bottles clinking. The passengers were about to hiss at us and tell us to behave, but the sight of our puffy faces covered in stubble made them decide to leave us alone. Andrei got into a quarrel with the conductress, who wanted us to pay for carrying luggage, and I started feeling unwell. So unwell that I couldn't stay

in that enclosed space any longer, crushed from all sides by backs
and elbows. I felt I was about to be sick and made a dash for the
door. My hands were holding the bags, so I used my shoulders and
stepped on a few people's feet.

"Stop, please, I'm feeling unwell!"

"I can't," the young woman at the wheel said without even
looking at me. "Wait until the stop."

"Of course you can! You just turn the wheel to the left and step
on the brake pedal!" I said furiously: I could clearly sense that the
critical moment was imminent. "Otherwise you'll be looking at the
contents of my stomach!"

The trolleybus reluctantly halted and I threw myself out through
the open doors. One bag got stuck between two passengers and
remained inside, the other was in front of me, so I couldn't see what
I was stepping on. It was a track of pure ice, polished by thousands of
braking wheels. I flung my arms up in the air as I crashed awkwardly
on to my backside. The first thing I heard was the sound of breaking
glass, and that was followed by laughter from everyone in the
trolleybus. Outraged, I tried to get up, but failed completely: my
hands and feet skidded away from each other, and the more furiously
I moved, the more clearly I realised the futility of my efforts and the
absurdity of my situation, and that made me absolutely furious. I
had to turn over on to my stomach and get up on to all fours. From
this pose on the ice rink, I began hurling streams of curses at the
trolleybus driver. It is quite possible that even the passers-by and
the passengers were astounded by the limitless riches of Russian
obscenity. The central idea of my address came down to the fact that,
unlike male drivers, who brake smoothly and repeatedly, stupid
women behind the wheel only press the brake once, as far as it will
go, thereby transforming the streets into ice-skating rinks. I still

hadn't finished speaking when the trolleybus calmly closed its doors and moved on. Beside myself with rage and burning with shame, I crept towards a roadside pillar, dragging the bag of broken glass behind me.

I was so furious with myself and the entire world, but above all with that trolleybus driver, that I completely forgot I had been feeling sick and all I wanted was revenge for my humiliation. I wanted to explain to that stupid girl that she might drive a big vehicle, but she was supposed to be serving people, and people need to be treated like human beings. After lunch, when Andrei and I had finally had our cold beer and I'd extorted from him where the controller's office for route 17 was, I set off for Gagarin Street. I ought to add that, owing to my confrontational personality, workers in the service sector usually hate me. For instance, in order to attract the attention of shop assistants who pretend not to notice me, I start singing in a loud voice. And when waiters are slow or simply don't want to bring me the bill, I say to them: "I hope you won't take offence if I offer you a little money?" And, of course, acting on the principle that "the world should strive towards perfection", I never let slip a chance to write some mean comment or other in the complaints book.

From her colleagues at the turning circle I learned that two girls drove the light green number 17 trolleybus – Katya and Liza, who for some reason everybody called Lizka. And when the trolleybus came back after completing its route, and this Lizka – I recognised her immediately – went off towards the controller's office, I walked in behind her.

I'm one of those people who only think really well when they're talking. In my words, the story I told her colleagues accumulated such a dense mass of accusations that it sounded as if Lizka had committed a crime against humanity. I described in lurid detail how the throwing out on to the black ice of an unfortunate, defenceless passenger had provoked a massive traffic accident involving at least twenty vehicles. The traffic would be paralysed for two days, the hospitals couldn't cope with the flood of victims, trolleybus depot number 4 would be bankrupted after the courts made it pay everyone for the physical and moral harm they had suffered. For some reason – evidently the sixth mug of beer had been one too many – I even quoted a friend of mine, also a poet, who had recently published a book of verse for children about the highway code.

However, her boss was only interested in something quite different, to whit: why the driver had halted her vehicle where there was no stop. Prodding Lizka furiously with his finger, he wanted to know if she thought she was working on a taxi and, as well as that, he reminded her of all her old sins and promised me that the question of her dismissal would be considered immediately and the decision would very probably be in favour.

As God is my witness, that wasn't what I'd wanted. The girl stood there in front of me, staring blankly like a child, without making any excuses or raising any objections. Two thoughts ran through my head. I won't mention the first one, because every man thinks about that at least six times every hour. But as well as that, I also wondered why I'd chosen her as the target for my attack, and I immediately realised how stupid I'd been, and now someone entirely innocent might suffer as a result.

That evening Andrei gave me the answer to my question. He'd put his video recorder in hock so that we could spend the evening with a bottle or two of Madeira, and in order to provide me with the money I needed to go back home. Andrei believed that my outburst of aggression was nothing less than a disguised protest against reality. My personal humiliation had been the final straw against the background of general humiliation by the machine of oppression, i.e., the state. Regardless of whether you had a good job or a bad one, you were still paid a miserly wage, and it only arrived several months late: the staffing levels of the militia were increasing proportionately to the dissatisfaction of the citizens, as expressed in meetings and strikes; idiotic centralisation meant that every meaningless detail had to be agreed with Moscow; weekly price hikes had confused everyone, and no one could say for certain anymore how much anything cost in roubles, so everyone counted in hard currency; men gave the army offices a wide berth, because they were looking for cannon fodder for their unnecessary wars; the state bureaucrats' wages had been doubled so that they would have no motive for corruption, and now they demanded bribes that were double the size as well; and with all this going on, the feeling never left you that you were a nobody with no rights. It was forbidden to organise a revolution, and anyway everybody was already tired of them; you were fed up of waiting and meditating, and especially of listening to warnings from hypocrites who didn't want you to do anything: "Have patience, don't do anything, accept reality!" they shouted. And what were people who were incapable of existing mindlessly, and who therefore did not wish to accept things, supposed to do?

And the saddest thing of all was that people were reading their newspapers and magazines and had stopped reading poetry altogether. But Lizka had absolutely nothing to do with all that.

We spent the entire night talking about poetry, or rather, about the technical side of poetastering, and as morning came my friend assured me that even though he wasn't printed either, he still had influential friends who wouldn't allow Lizka to be sacked.

My guilty conscience wouldn't allow me to leave G. without apologising to Lizka. I wondered for a long time what present to give her in order to make up for things, and finally settled on a pair of house slippers in the form of two funny plush rabbits.

I walked unhurriedly through the city with its dusting of fresh snow, holding the box with the slippers under my arm and wondering how I could start the conversation with her, and whether she would want to talk to me at all. The hangover syndrome had gradually released me from its grip, and I was in an excellent mood. After the binge, the world had once more acquired its former attractiveness; everything had become precise, clear and simple, and therefore incredibly funny. Somewhere in some corner of my mind the idea was born of writing a poem about summer. If I was going to write about summer, I had to do it in winter, because in summer I was tormented by the heat, the dust and the wasps.

I had almost reached the office of Lizka's controller when a young man with a stick suddenly came leaping up to me and knocked me down. I tried to get up, but he wouldn't let me and began beating me furiously with his stick, so that I started howling with the pain, covering my head with my hands. Then he leaned down over me, squeezing my neck hard in his hands and hissed: "You leave her alone. She belongs to me!"

He had terrifying, wild eyes and the yellow teeth of a smoker, with saliva splattering through them. Grabbing hold of my collar, he set me on my feet in a single jerk and limped away. Then he turned back and added: "If I ever see you here again, I'll kill you!"

I didn't understand what this man wanted from me. And apart from that, I wasn't thinking too clearly because of the sharp pain in my side; I just watched the bright red blood dripping out of my nose on to the white snow.

"Are you hurt?" asked an elderly man who had stopped in front of me. "Shall I call an ambulance?"

"Yes, please."

He took out a mobile phone and rang for an ambulance, then he helped me lower myself into a snowdrift, picked up the box and gave me a handkerchief.

"Who did this to you?"

"I have no idea."

"You'd better not move, your ribs might be broken."

He was right. The doctor told me I really did have a broken rib and bound me up tightly with an elastic bandage, assuring me that it would definitely knit together. And as well as that, he diagnosed concussion and said he was going to keep me in for five days. So the funny fluffy-rabbit slippers came in very handy. They were too small for me, of course, and my heels were always touching the floor, but I think that I cut a very elegant figure in hospital pyjamas and those slippers. Being in hospital certainly has its own pleasures. They look after you, it's quiet everywhere, you only have to get up for lunch. And apart from that, you hear so many different life stories from your neighbours in the other beds that your own life starts to seem quite ordinary.

I had three visits quite soon. The first to call in was Andrei, delighted that I was going to be delayed in his city a bit longer. So that I wouldn't be bored, he gave me a book by Freud, with the following inscription: "Grandpa Freud tried everything in life, and everything he didn't like he categorised as perversion. May you, my brother poet, also try everything." He's always recommending to me to spend some time in prison, or go to war, so that I might finally start writing good poetry, whereas I actually prefer an armchair and the television.

Then the local militiaman came and asked me in detail about

the man who had attacked me and drew up a report. The third visitor was Lizka.

"Hello, I've brought you some apples," she said, holding the bag out to me. "What's your name?"

"Kostya."

"I'm Lizka."

"I know. Wouldn't you like to sit down?"

She nodded. We went out into the corridor and made ourselves comfortable on the small couch by the wall. I felt rather awkward as I tried to guess the purpose of her visit. Of course, it was kind of her to enquire after my health, but how had she found out? Lizka looked down at the floor, then her glance moved to my slippers and the corners of her mouth twitched, but she hid her smile. The silence dragged on.

"By the way, you won't get the sack, you don't have to worry." I said the first thing that came into my head.

"Yes, they told me already. But what did you have to play out that drunken farce for, anyway? It was all your fault. It wasn't because of the broken bottles, was it?"

"No, it wasn't because of the bottles, just a crisis in my creative work."

"Are you a poet?"

"Yes."

"That's hard to believe. Poets don't take trolleybuses to cash in their bottles."

"Of course they do, poets are always cashing in their bottles because they've got no more room left for them. Those are the two most important things they do with their lives – write poems and ride in trolleybuses to cash in their bottles."

"I think you look more like a slob. I don't believe you're a poet."

"Do you want me to prove it?"

"Try."

I recited several lines about love by Lermontov, which I had learned off by heart.

"Beautiful," said Lizka.

"Yes," I agreed.

"Tell me, Kostya, has the local militiaman already been to see you?" she suddenly asked.

I nodded.

"Then soon the investigator will come and ask you to write an application for the criminal prosecution of Max Shmyrin."

"Who?"

"You know, it was Max who beat you up, because he was jealous about me."

"Is he a friend of yours?"

"No."

"Your husband?"

"No."

I thought I'd already guessed what had happened, but her answers confused me again. I looked at her quizzically.

"I feel awkward, because two people suddenly have problems because of me. Only you'll soon recover, and Max could end up in prison," she began, and went on to tell me the story of her relationship with Max, in which I had become an unwilling participant.

She asked me not to write a complaint and to pretend not to recognise Max if the investigator showed me his photo. She said he already had a long list of offences, so the judgement of the court could be very harsh. Having listened to Lizka's touching story, I agreed to do as she asked, and in my own mind I regretted that I didn't know how to write love novels.

"Listen, Lizka, have you noticed that this is the third time we've met in strange circumstances? Let's meet some time in normal surroundings, in a café or a park," I suggested, and immediately saw the mistrust in her eyes.

"Then I'll be able to tell you how everything went with the investigator."

"All right. Wednesday's my day off," she told me, and we said goodbye.

Ah, Kostya, Kostya! Why do you lie like that to yourself and other people? "Then I'll be able to tell you how everything went with the investigator." You noticed those love vibes in the air – those bright little stars, circling round the couch where the two of you were just sitting. Those stars were dashing backwards and forwards higgledy-piggledy between you and Lizka, trailing fuzzy little tails behind them, just like little comets. And surely you saw the snowdrops on the window on the other side of the corridor freeze in the air, forming the outline of a heart against the grey wall of the next building? And you won't punish the man who attacked you, not because you're so very noble, but because you don't want to upset her. You've fallen in love, Kostya, and it's not just an animal passion, your rib's too painful for that. And Lizka must have noticed those love vibes too, because she told you Wednesday is her day off.

You're lying to yourself again, Kostya. All the time she was talking about Max, you were staring at her knees, hidden under those woolly tights. And when you recited someone else's poem to her, you almost gobbled up her slim neck and the lobe of her ear with your eyes. What makes you any better than a male gibbon, Kostya?

I didn't have a good answer to that, so I carried on thinking.

It would be interesting to find out what she was like, this Lizka.

Maybe she was like my former girlfriend, who irritated me with her extravagant whimsy, constant cackling and hysterics, and who tried to take away what is most sacred to me – my armchair and television? It would be even worse if she was one of those women who are like men, who have already explained the world to themselves and therefore fling labels and prejudices around at every opportunity. And what if what was important to her was not to love, but to be loved? Then she could become a good mother, a custodian of the hearth and home, and I would die of boredom.

And the more I thought about her, the stronger my need and desire to see her again grew.

At our next meeting, I wanted to pull the wool over her eyes. What's so good about a poet telling a girl that he despises delicacies and expensive wines simply because he has no money to pay for them? Of course, I could make myself out to be a romantic, admiring the evening lights of the city from the roof of a high-rise building and reading poetry at the same time. I could even ride down a children's slide with her in a cardboard box from a television, holding my bad rib with my hand. But how would she look at me if I turned my pockets out and showed her just enough small change to pay for a tram-ride and a condom? And so, when I got out of hospital and went back to Andrei's house, instead of saying "hello", I threw a question at him: "Where can we get some money? It's your city, you must know."

Andrei frowned, dug around in the ashtray, found a largish cigarette butt and lit up.

"Our chemical combine has been converted and now it's making toothpaste," he said in an oddly morose manner. "If we write a good video clip for the local TV, we can earn two hundred dollars. Shall we write one?"

What a humiliation for a creative artist, to advertise toothpaste, I thought, and I shouted: "Of course!"

This toothpaste had an indeterminate colour and a strange taste, it bore the name "Chemowhite" and, in Andrei's opinion, it was very good for bleaching toilet bowls. After two days and nights of torment, we presented the results of our labours to the marketing department of the chemical combine. In our script, a group of people travelling through the jungle were walking across a log over a river when one of them fell off, but at the same time a tube of "Chemowhite" fell out of his pocket, and while the computer-generated or cartoon piranhas were busy cleaning their teeth with it and grinning brightly, he managed to swim to the bank. However, the client declared that the local TV wasn't Hollywood, and he needed something a bit simpler and a bit cheaper. We had a reserve version – a girl strolling through a park with a green piglet on a lead, with a voice-over saying: "We don't know what the pets of the future will be like, but we do know for certain that everybody will be using 'Chemowhite.'" The client thought he detected a negative hint at the plant's previous product lines in this, but we eventually managed to get him to agree that a green piglet was the best possible symbol for this product and he paid us, although he only paid half of the money.

There are probably cities and countries where fifty dollars isn't very much money, but in G. it was a week of delightful pleasures and half of Lizka's monthly pay. Sleigh-riding with a fast troika of horses, examining the little freaks in the museum of curiosities, and dinner in an elite restaurant that still had doormen in livery and classic cuisine – those are the sorts of things that can bring people closer in just one day. I told Lizka how our Chukchi run across the Bering Strait to the American Eskimos to exchange fur for carbines, why the police couldn't find the underground Chinese factory producing "Rolex" watches, how the priests left their churches through an underground passage if there was any danger, and all sorts of other cheerful nonsense. Her mistrust and caution gradually evaporated and her eyes started to glow with curiosity. At first she only seemed to smile reluctantly, like a sulky child, but then she couldn't hold out anymore and she burst into spontaneous peals of laughter and took hold of my hand for the first time. With that boisterous laughter, that little snub nose in her face turned rosy by the frost, that lively sparkle in her brown eyes, those slim, shapely legs under her clumsily tailored coat – how lovely she was in all her naturalness! A good hairdresser and a beauty parlour would have transformed her into a real beauty – if only it were possible afterwards not to take her over to the mirror and tell her how beautiful she was, so that the inevitable mask of arrogance wouldn't spoil her genuine loveliness.

We spent the next few evenings in discotheques and bars and went to the cinema. Once she thought that she'd seen Max. I tensed up in readiness for a fight, and was grateful when Lizka suggested that we should escape from him in a taxi. Fate probably intended this obstacle to being us closer together, and on the back seat of the taxi we kissed for the first time.

I shared my impressions of Lizka with Andrei, adding that I'd been looking for girlfriend for a long-term relationship, maybe even someone to marry, for a long time.

"You're not thinking of getting married now, are you?" he asked suspiciously.

"And why not?"

"For a poet marriage is tantamount to suicide."

"We still won't have enough money to publish in *samizdat*."

"No, you won't. Only the constant state of being in love and, therefore, insane, can serve as the source of creative energy. And apart from that, we have such a wide choice. Because our country has had too many wars and revolutions, the ratio of women to men is two to one. If we exclude all the lovers of vodka, then for every man there are three women. So what's the hurry? My fiancée, for instance, is still in the ninth class at school. Sometimes I visit the school and enquire what kind of marks my future wife is getting, and what hobby groups she goes too."

"I don't know, Andrei, but Lizka's kind of…"

"Kind of what?"

"She's not like all the walking corpses that I've met so far."

Andrei must have spotted the dreamy expression in my eyes, because he just waved his hand at me despairingly and growled: "I bought you a ticket for the train."

"Thanks."

On the last night before I was going away, I lay on the bed in Lizka's room with my hands behind my head, examining the cracks in the ceiling. She came back from the bathroom, dived under the blanket and pressed her cheek against mine, breathing a strong smell of tobacco over me.

"Why don't you give up smoking?" I asked her. "Your teeth are already yellow as it is. And anyway, do you know how many people die prematurely from lung cancer?"

Lizka jumped up and turned away from me.

"Listen," she said, and suddenly started getting dressed. "I don't want any commitments. Sex is no excuse for getting too familiar, and all that, do you understand?"

"Are you trying to tell me that we're not going to carry on with this?"

"No, we're not. Go away."

"Hey, is all this just because I don't like you smoking?" I tried to catch hold of her hand, but she moved away.

"You courted me in style, I slept with you. You got what you wanted, now leave me in peace," Lizka said, and threw my trousers at me. "I don't want to see you again!"

"But I thought we'd make a rather good couple," I objected.

"You're just like all the rest! You're all smug, self-assured rats, swines and bastards! I hate you!"

While I was getting dressed, she stood over by the window and smoked nervously, blowing the smoke out through the small open ventilator window. I tried to put my arms round her shoulders, but she turned away sharply and shouted with tears in her eyes.

"Get out! Out! You can't even imagine how much I hate you!"

I left.

EPILOGUE

VICTOR MIKHAILOVICH BECAME governor. His black limousine with tinted windows and a blue flashing light on the roof occasionally went hurtling through the streets of G., accompanied by a police escort. He explained to the striking workers that they needed to have patience, because the country was passing though a temporary crisis. A journalist asked him spitefully, "Why do you work with bandits?"

"Why do you call them bandits?" Victor Mikhalovich replied with a condescending smile. "They used to be bandits before, but now they're major entrepreneurs, Russia's greatest hope and support, so to speak. Just yesterday I asked them to build a children's hospital, and I'm sure they'll definitely do it."

Only very recently he was involved in a big scandal in the press. The governor visited a piggery on some collective farm and was photographed beside two stud boars. One of the newspapers printed this photograph with the legend: "Our governor Victor Mikhailovich is the third from the right." This newspaper's offices were later closed down when they were accused of keeping hard drugs on the premises.

Katya and Artur are living together and still working at trolleybus depot number 4. Artur has taken on route 17, so now they're partners. They say Katya's expecting his child, and he keeps paying more and more signs of attention to his conductress Liubasha, but she doesn't take any notice.

The doctor Zoya Andreevna and Vera's conductress Irina have joined a crochet circle.

Vera herself is still living her double life, and giving no sign at all that it doesn't suit her. Recently she got her husband to give her a new BMW and became a member of the city's female parachuting team.

Nina married her neighbour, the plumber Tolya, and now they have their own separate room in the same old hostel.

As for Lizka and me, we moved to my home city and got married. I won't say which city it is. Because of Max. He broke a militiaman's arm and he was put away for two years. We wouldn't like him to find us when he's let out.

Lizka now works as an instructor in a private driving school. Over dinner she always tells me what useless drivers men are and says that if she had her way, she wouldn't give half of her pupils a licence. Her constant indignation and moaning irritate me so much that I lock myself away from her in my room and remind her through the door that she shouldn't get worked up, because she's already more than a month gone.

My collection of lyrical verses "with something about the moon and a woman's bare breast" has finally been published. The critics, of course, absolutely panned it, and even Andrei and Stepanich mocked my four-foot iambic metre, but people read it and say they like it.

It's hard for me to say exactly what it is in Lizka that attracts me; perhaps it's simply her youth, or perhaps it's the freshness that she has preserved, despite all the changes life has put her through, but I know that we'll easily manage to overcome the first, and even the second, crisis in our relationship – by withdrawing into ourselves and not separating, but maintaining our friendship and consideration for each other until the next upsurge of feelings. It seems to me that with the wife I have found we can be lovers, comrades-in-arms and friends for the rest of our lives. I just wonder whether she thinks the same. Sometimes in the evening, when I settle down in a comfortable armchair to watch the ice hockey, she leaves the flat without saying a word, silently closing the door behind her. I look at the funny, pink fluffy-rabbit slippers she has left behind and wonder if she's going to come back.